Ladies' Lunch

AND OTHER STORIES

Sort Of Books, PO Box 18678, London NW3 2FL

Typeset in Garamond to a design by Henry Iles

Distributed by Profile Books
29 Cloth Fair, London EC1A 7JQ

1 3 5 7 9 10 8 6 4 2

A catalogue record for this book is available
from the British Library
ISBN 978-1914502033

Printed and bound by CPI Group (UK) Ltd, Croydon, CR0 4YY

Ladies' Lunch

AND OTHER STORIES

LORE SEGAL

Sort Of
BOOKS

To the "Ladies"
the real and the imagined,
Dee, Inea, Leina, Sheila, Susan

Lore Segal, New York, January 2023

Contents

LADIES' LUNCH

1

Ruth, Frank and Dario

The February ladies' lunch met at Ruth's Riverside apartment. "Ladies' lunch" is pronounced in quotation marks. The five women have grown old coming together, every other month or so, for the last thirty or more years, around one another's tables. Ruth, Bridget, Farah, Lotte, Bessie are long-time New Yorkers; their origins in California, County Mayo, Tehran, Vienna and the Bronx might have grounded them but does not these days often surface.

"You remember," Ruth said, "that we are the people to whom we tell our stories? Well, I have a story for you."

"Great," said Lotte.

"Good," said Farah and Bessie.

"A number of stories," Ruth told them, "and at the end there is a puzzle."

"Good egg," said Bridget.

Ruth said:

There was this party at Sylvia's that turned out to be a shivah for her cousin. Sylvia came over and asked me should she get me a chair. I told her, "Thanks, very kind, but I'll find one when I need to sit."

"Get you a drink?" she said.

I told her, "Sylvia! I can manage. Honestly. The cane is for balance."

"And I should stop fussing and go away?"

"You don't have to go away." We laughed and Sylvia said she hoped it was OK that she had given Frank my number. He was dying to talk to me.

"Frank? Which Frank is this?"

"Ruth, you know Frank Bruno."

"Frank Bruno, yes, oh, I think it's that I think of him as Bruno Frank."

Sylvia said, "Frank works in a gallery on Bleecker Street and wants to know about your old buddy, your client – what was Dario d'Alessi? Anyhow he wants to talk to you."

"So why doesn't he walk over and talk?"

Sylvia said, "He says he's afraid of you."

I was annoyed. "That is such nonsense. What does it even mean? Where is he?"

"Over there," said Sylvia, "walking out the door."

It had irritated her, Ruth told the friends, at lunch, to find herself waiting for Frank to call. The prospect of telling her old Dario stories, she said, had opened a window onto such a chunk of time. She called Sylvia and asked for Bruno's number.

"Bruno?" Sylvia said. "Which Bruno is this?"

"Frank. I mean, Frank Bruno who wants to talk to me."

Ruth had dialled and hung up because she couldn't think, at the moment, if it was Bruno, or Frank. Frank. She dialled. "Frank, this is Ruth. Your asking about Dario d'Alessi has started all these stories in my head."

Frank said, "That's what I hoped! God! That's what I want. I Googled you. You were Dario d'Alessi's lawyer."

"I was," she had told him. "There was paperwork to do with the people he hired to fabricate – 'fabricate', that was the word – one of his sculptures. I got to go upstate with him into this sort of hangar where men were working on a twenty-foot black curl. I was never happier. I loved listening to the craftsmen talking with each other."

"God!" Frank said. "How did you meet him?"

Ruth said, "I was one of the groupies who hung around whenever he came to New York. Years later, I visited him in the Italian Alps, in his place. It was like a Mesa Verde cave dwelling, if you can imagine a Bauhaus cave carved out of the Italian mountainside. Did you know him?"

"Me. No! No," Frank said. "I saw him once coming out of a restaurant on East 17th Street and I walked behind him for a number of blocks. He went into a grocery and I watched him through the window. He came out, went into a liquor store and bought a bottle. Then he got into a bus going west."

Ruth told her friends, "I had the thrill of thinking: so that's what Dario did on the way over to my place – like watching a scene happening thirty years ago. But then Frank said he'd been in his twenties and too shy to catch up and tell this man that he loved his show – so it must have been Dario's early show, years before the one-man at the Guggenheim, before I even knew him. I told Frank that Dario might have been grateful. He used to talk about the desolation of that early success and his first New York visit before he knew people."

Frank said the gallery had just acquired a d'Alessi.

"Which one?"

"Called 'Hatch'."

"I remember, I remember! Oh, oh, I remember the bunch of us sitting with a bottle of Malbec trying to come up with a name for a new d'Alessi piece, to replace 'Untitled'. It had to be what Clement Greenberg called a word 'independent of meaning', in the days when our favourite cartoon was a museum-goer wiping a tender tear in front of a Russian constructivist sculpture. You don't know till you try how hard it is to think of words that signify no object, or feeling, or value ... I'd wake up in the night with the sense of triumph: 'Bout!' – but that means 'strife'. 'Upstanding' got shot down because it commented on 'standing down'. There are so many stories!" I said.

Frank said that I was a resource and asked if he could take me to lunch, but the day of the lunch he called for a raincheck. Major snafu at the gallery. I've invited him up for a drink.

The March ladies' lunch went out to Bessie's in Old Rockingham. Frank Bruno had not made it to Ruth's for that drink. Someone from the gallery called. Frank was out of state and would call as soon as he got back.

The friends said, "Tell us the d'Alessi stories you were going to tell Frank Bruno."

Ruth said, "Here's something I didn't understand when I was visiting Dario. I called his attention to a man, a farmer, sitting on the pavement in the village square with a little goat on his lap. The man held the animal's hoof the way you might hold a child's, or a young girl's hand. Dario said, 'He's going to take the goat to be slaughtered,' which I always remembered afterwards, the way you remember something that doesn't add up."

Ruth said, "Dario took me on a climb. He climbed like a mountaineer – one foot after another at an even pace. I impressed myself by overtaking him. Then I had to sit down and recover my breath while he moved steadily on and up.

"And the terrifying drive up the mountain road to see the oldest houses on the highest range. You have to understand that Dario was the world's worst driver. And on the way back we ran out of petrol. Because you are statistically more likely to come upon a wayside crucifix memorialising someone's plunge to death than a gas pump, the locals – unlike Dario – drive with a spare can of gas. Dario and I sat with the car door open and we sat and we sat until the milkman's truck came up the road. The milkman syphoned off enough gas to get us back to Altomonte. Dario took out his wallet. I had enough Italian to understand that the milkman said 'No, no no, no grazie! Signor Dario, no! Che mi faccia un autografo.' I wondered how many upstate New York milkmen would prefer a de Kooning or a Rothko signature to a couple of twenties."

At Farah's lunch in April, Ruth reported that Frank Bruno had cancelled another appointment – the friends began to smile – one of those spring colds that are so famously hard to shake.

"Ruth," Farah, asked her, "Are you annoyed with him?"

Ruth said, "I would have said no way, except that I'm telling you about it."

Bessie's husband, Colin, was not well, so she did not come to the May lunch at Lotte's.

Frank had had to go and get a grown son out of some snafu and hadn't made it to the latest appointment.

Here was the puzzle, and it engaged the four friends' powers of speculation.

Lotte said, "First thing, if someone tells you they have a snafu, a cold, a son, is to believe them."

Farah said, "One can imagine a twenty-year-old too shy to approach a man with a famous name, but what stops the middle-aged New Yorker from crossing the room to speak to a woman?"

"An old woman," Ruth said.

"At a New York party," said Lotte.

"A New York shivah," Ruth said.

The June ladies' lunch met at Bridget's. Frank had not made it to Ruth's place and Bridget said *she* had a story:

"I asked my delightful twenty-year-old niece, Lily, if she remembers refusing to come into the house if my ninety-year-old mother was in. Lily says she remembers that my mother wore the earpiece of her glasses *across* her ear instead of tucked behind the ear and she had been afraid. She remembers crying and not wanting to come in."

"Lily was how old?" asked Lotte.

"Six years, maybe."

"And how does that throw light on a grown man not talking to Ruth at a party?"

"At a shivah," Ruth said.

Bridget said, "Just another story that doesn't add up."

The ladies' lunch met back at Ruth's early in July, before everybody dispersed for the summer. No, Frank had not come. Frank had called...

The friends began to smile.

"Frank said that there was a fire, in the apartment next to his apartment."

The friends laughed.

Bridget said, "Maybe there really was a fire?"

"It's possible," Ruth said.

2

Days of Martini and Forgetting

*How pleasant the sight of a
cheerful old person.*

ANON

"Love your stole," Lotte said to the handsome old woman at the party, "it's grand and beautiful." The woman thanked Lotte while her eyes flicked subliminally to the left: she did not recognise Lotte, nor could Lotte abort the identical tell on her own face. To save her children's heads she could not have said if she had forgotten the woman's name or had never laid eyes on her. Lotte walked with a cane and the woman in the stole offered to get her a drink.

"Oh, thanks, no, I'm fine, really," Lotte told her. "I can get it myself."

Lotte was happy to see Bessie by the coat rack and walked over. Bessie said, "I'm going to stow my cane. It has a way of tripping people."

"You made it in from Rockingham," Lotte said.

"Made it in," Bessie said.

"How is Colin?"

"Colin is well – well enough. Colin is all right."

Bessie must have known that her friends could not stand Colin, the only one of the husbands still living. Colin owned houses, cars, talked about the inadequacy of the parking and was dying of something slow and ravaging.

"Who is the old woman in the red stole?" Lotte asked Bessie.

"Cynthia," said Bessie, "your hostess."

And then Bessie added that she was surprised to see Lotte.

"Why are you surprised? The third time I called to ask you for the address, you were understandably irritable."

"And you said you were not going."

"Yes, well," Lotte said, "the prospect of leaving my apartment brings on an initial desire to take my Kindle and go to bed. A small agoraphobia, but I like parties."

"If you want to call it a party. I hope they do martinis."

"Why isn't it a party?" asked Lotte, following her friend, who seemed to know the geography of the handsome modern apartment.

They were intercepted by an unusually large young man – a younger man, at any rate – who kissed Bessie and asked, "Has anybody seen Cynthia?"

"Who was that?" Lotte asked Bessie.

"Don't know," said Bessie. "Reminds me of the seventies when one kept getting hugged by students who had come out from behind their beards."

"And who is Cynthia?"

"Your hostess. The woman in the stole," Bessie said.

Drinks were in the kitchen where Bessie was drawn into conversation with people she knew. Lotte put out a hand to an old man standing by himself. She said, "My late husband and I had an agreement: every party we went to we would talk to at least one person we didn't know."

"And today is my lucky day." The old man had a nice face.

"Those were the days…" said Lotte.

"Of wine and roses," the old man said.

"I was going to say the days when I used to know eighty percent of the people at a party. Today I know two people."

"That's doing better than I by one," he said. "Tell me the two you know."

"My friend Bessie, whom I've known for over half a century, and the woman in the beautiful red stole, whom I just talked with."

"That's the one I know. She's my sister," said the man. "Ruthie was our aunt. I've come in from Albany."

A quarter-turn brought the large, younger man who had kissed Bessie into the conversation.

"We are talking about all the people we don't know," Lotte told him.

The younger man said, "I'm developing an algorithm that will interpret the musculature of the face of the persons you're talking with and tell you who they are and how you know them."

Bessie came with martinis, for Lotte and herself. She said, "Let's sit down. I can't stand so long."

"And just in time; I've used up my conversation starters," Lotte told her.

They carried their drinks to a comfortable sofa and sat down. Lotte asked Bessie, "One more time tell me the name of our hostess."

"Cynthia."

"I talked with her brother..."

"Sebastian," said Bessie.

"Who is Ruthie?"

"Ruth Berger," said Bessie, "Cynthia and Sebastian's aunt, who always reminded me of that *New Yorker* cartoon: 'That is Mortimer her first husband and her second novel.' And you still like parties?" Bessie asked Lotte.

"I do."

Bessie said, "I remember when we used to go in expectation, always, that something – that somebody – was going to happen. What do I get dressed for today? What do I come in from Old Rockingham for?"

"People," said Lotte. "Conversation."

"And have you had a good conversation today?"

"Not that kind of conversation. It's like the old balls – you take a turn with one partner and take a turn with another partner."

"And you're having a good time?"

"Yes, I am."

Bessie was looking around the room. The set of her face told Lotte that Colin was not all right. "What makes today good for you?" Bessie asked Lotte.

"Let's see. For one, my children, so far as I know, are well and are modestly solvent. Two, right knee doesn't hurt. Three, I enjoyed looking at – what's her name again?"

"Cynthia."

"…looking at Cynthia's splendid red stole, and her brother..?"

"Sebastian."

"...has a nice face. I like being in these handsome rooms, and sitting on a comfortable sofa, drinking a good martini. I like talking with you with the sound of a party in back of me."

"The sound of a shivah," said Bessie.

"Another shivah? Whose shivah?"

Bessie said, "This is the shivah for Cynthia and Sebastian's aunt, Ruth Berger."

"It is!"

"Who said that wakes and funerals are the cocktail parties of the old?"

3

How Lotte Lost Bessie

Old friends bound by the closest ties of mental sympathy will cease, after a certain year, to make the necessary journey or even cross the street to see one another.

MARCEL PROUST

BESSIE, DEAR FRIEND—

Let me understand for which of my crimes I am to be punished by your failing to see me, your managing to not hear me calling you – don't we hear our own name even if we happen to be milling up the aisle in a crowded concert? Why, by the way, didn't you let me know that you were coming to town? Where are you staying? I had to actually touch your elbow and then, of course, we were all smiles – and those little exclamations on my part, of the sheer pleasure, always, of seeing you. Or did you simply not see me sitting in the row on your left, three places in? Our eyes aren't as quick as they used to be, it's true, and you were busy looking for a seat. You didn't take the empty place next to mine because, it turned out, you were not alone.

"You remember Anstiss," you informed me. I'm not so good these days with names, but one isn't likely to forget Anstiss, a class act – she must be in her mid-nineties – half a head taller than you or I. She said, "I showed you around my Old Rockingham house." You said, "The house next to Colin's on the right, that Colin wanted you to buy." I should not have said, "To give him access to the parking area," and added, "totally mistaking the sorry state of my finances." You said, "Did I tell you we've bought a little pied-à-terre in Manhattan?" "You did not tell me," I said. You did not invite me to come with you and Anstiss to find seats together.

What didn't we used to do together, Bessie, you and Eli, and Matthew and I: our Friday night movies, Thanksgivings, Seders. How many New Years did we survive together, and every summer all the way back to our trip to Venice on the day the last of our foursome finished the last of the examinations? That vaporetto, empty except for three Dutch students attached to overstuffed backpacks, and the beautiful Venetian grandmother. You said her hair and gown were the colour of pewter. The little grandson had arrived on our late flight and went to sleep with his head on her lap. "I can't believe you actually live here!" I said to her. She pointed through a gap on the left, at her house, the Palazzo Zevi. I think we were waiting for her to invite us. She told us where to get off and how to find our hotel.

The thrill, the romance just of lugging our bags through empty Venetian streets, nobody left awake except for that party of pleasantly drunk young men sitting under a garland of vines round a table outside a closed taverna. Their shirts were the colour of moons. One rose, lofted his full glass for a beacon and walked us around two corners to the small hotel. That, too, was closed for the night. Through a glass inset, I could see the clerk sit up on his folding cot, brace his elbows on his lap, set his chin on the heels of his hands and go back to sleep. Our Venetian young man banged on the door in Italian until the clerk came to hand us our keys and plumped back down on his cot. Our Venetian in the moon-shirt returned, we supposed, to his friends under the vines and we bumped our bags up the stairs and fell finally into our beds.

You and I – we loved it that our men were liking each other. My Matt made up for his five foot something with his continual jokes. Couldn't help it. He estimated every third to be a hit, and his project, he said, was to abort the misses in between. Eli's project was to grow a beard, which, at that juncture, didn't, as I remember, promise well.

And, Bessie, the gondola passing the wall pocked and striated by water, weather, time. Eli said, "The grandmother didn't invite us into her palazzo because Venetian palazzi do not have insides." Matt said, "But it has another façade where a gondola is passing on another canal." I can't tell you whether that's as rich as I thought it then, think it now. I was in love with the four of us. Curious, no? I would have staked my life – do stake my life – on our friendship persisting into our old age!

Because the guys were bent over the map, they never saw the door open and a servant put a foot out onto the moss-covered, water-lapped stepping stone. You and I looked through the opening to the garden inside the nonexistent dimension where giant fronds growing out of a white marble bath cascaded to the terrace below. You said they were the same sharp green as the bug you kept in a matchbox, when you were a child, and that it had died. The servant, having given the bucket that final swirl which doesn't ever entirely empty what is in the bottom, took a backward step and shut the door.

You married Eli. Matthew and I married and watched the two of you getting on each other's nerves, though you were beautiful – you stuck by us. No brother and sister could have hung closer through the terrible, long year of Matthew's dying.

Eli remembers that you originally intended Colin for me, because you couldn't bear me to be sad and alone. "He is large and beautiful and owns a boat," you told me. "We're all going to his place in Connecticut for the weekend." "Not me," I said. "Yes! You, you!" you said. "And he owns a house in Aix-en-Provence." I refrained from asking what you knew of me that made you imagine I could stomach Colin Woodworth. Or did I fail to refrain? I remember your looking disappointed, your asking me, "You don't think he's gorgeous?" I said, "Colin has drawn me two alternate routes from my place to his house in Old Rockingham." "Well!" you said. "How beastly of him, to want to facilitate the drive for you!" Bessie! That silly, man-high wooden fence to prevent the pedestrians of Bay Street from sneaking a peek at Colin Woodworth's square of grass, like a toy garden kept inside the box it came in.

Oh, but the deck in back! It overlooked the great crinkled blue bay, the traffic of the boats like so many little white triangles. We lay on sun-warmed wood and drank martinis and I wished Colin would shut up about the new element in Old Rockingham to whom agreements, he said, weren't worth the paper they were written on. "What element would that be?" I asked him. Eli took the moment to stand up and wonder if anyone wanted to walk into the village. You said, "Colin means his pesty neighbour on the left." Colin said, "Like the Bainses in number eight. All they are out for is themselves." "In which," I said, "they probably resemble you and me and most everybody I know." "I don't know what you mean," Colin said, and he fetched out the fresh Polaroid showing the Bainses' Toyota openly, *brazenly* parked on the Woodworth side of an imaginary line which Colin's finger described down the centre of the parking area shared by the adjacent properties. I said, "But isn't that because I, in my ignorance, parked myself on the Bains side?" Eli asked you if you were coming for a walk or not. You said, "Not." Colin said, "It's provocation pure and simple. I've spoken to my lawyer in Boston."

In the car, driving home from that first visit, you said, "He's the perfect host." "Makes good martinis," I said. "The village is nice, if you like museums," Eli said. You said, "Well, I say he's sweet. At bottom he's a generous, affectionate man, don't you think?" "Colin Woodworth is an ass and you know it," I never should have said and I felt mean and a little guilty when Colin called to invite me for the following weekend sounding friendly and thoroughly nice. Said he was mailing me a map of an alternate to the alternate route that would cut twenty minutes at the least. I asked him if you and Eli were coming and he said, yes, you were coming.

I remember only the one conversation that you and I had on the subject of Colin. This was after you and Eli split and Eli had left for London. You came to tell me you were moving to Connecticut: "Why should you be surprised that I could love a person who might not suit your taste? I think he is a dear man." "I'm sure he is that, to you," I said. "I can see he is." "If only that he likes me, which is a nice change from Eli." "Well, I intend to like Colin," I promised you, and promised myself. "I will. I'm going to like Colin for you." "And you'll come weekends," you said, "and you're coming to Provence with us next summer."

I try to think backward: When did you stop inviting me? When did I begin to be envious, to regret having no places to not invite *you* to? I don't know that I blame you because I was never nice to Colin, nor about him. (In our emails, Eli and I refer to him as Mr Collins.) You knew that the week in London I stayed with Eli. Funny how, afterwards, we could no longer sign off with the easy old "Love, Eli" and "Love, Lotte" – the word had become freighted. That was after you and Colin married, but of course I've wondered, sex being what it is, if it rankled. Rankles. Except that in all the years since then, you stay with me when you come up to town. We do the theatre and the parties Colin isn't keen on. And we talk. (Eli and I wonder what you and Mr Collins talk about besides the still-raging parking wars.)

You and I used to talk and talk. Wait. Hold on. I had to go and find Jane Austen. Here: this is Emma thinking about Mrs Weston, the friend "interested in every pleasure, every scheme of hers, to whom she could speak every thought as it arose." Bessie, that was you and me, until you learned to say, "Anyway," which being interpreted can only mean, "When you stop telling me what you are telling me, we can get back to what I was saying." And so now, dear Bessie, I think twice before speaking the thought as it arises, at a time of life when I'm as likely as not to forget a name, forget the operative word. Bessie! Are you so sure you mightn't want to hear what I might want to say? Or, Bessie, does it feel to you as if I am not listening to what you are saying?

I went to find you at intermission. We stood and we talked. That is to say, you and the ancient Anstiss sat in your seats and I stood. What rose in my mind to say was how you and Eli and Matt and I used to always go to hear – the name of what I couldn't remember. I asked what you and Anstiss were doing after the concert, and it seemed that you had arranged to meet some Old Rockingham people for a late dinner. You said, "I'll see you at ladies' lunch. I'll call you if I get to town before." "Wonderful!" I told you. Only give me some lead time." "Will do," you said, and I went back to my seat.

Outside, after the concert, I stood on the sidewalk, waiting to wave goodbye. You were surrounded by a small bustle of well-dressed, well-looking elderly couples, getting into cabs. You had your assisting hand under Anstiss's elbow. I could tell that you simply did not see me.

Here's something for us to talk about the next time: How simple is this "simply"? I'll give you a call.

Love,
Lotte

4

The Arbus Factor

On one of the first days of the New Year, Jack called Hope. "Let's have lunch. I've got an agenda," he said. No need to specify the Café Provence – nor the time – fifteen minutes before noon, when they were sure of getting their table by the window.

They did the menu, heard the specials. Hope said, "I'm always *going* to order something different," but ordered the onion soup. Jack ordered the cassoulet, saying, "I *should* have fish. And a bottle of your Merlot," he told the unsmiling proprietress, "which we will have right away."

"We'll share a salad," Hope said. She watched Jack watch the proprietress walk off in the direction of the bar: A remarkably short skirt for a woman of fifty. Hope saw the long, bare, brown, athletic legs with Jack's eyes.

Jack, a large man, with a dark, heavy face, now turned to Hope.

"So?"

"OK, I guess. You?"

Jack said, "My agenda: if we were still making resolutions, what would yours be?"

Hope's interest pricked right up. "I'm thinking. You go first."

Jack said, "Watch what I eat. It's not the weight, it's the constantly thinking of eating. I don't eat real meals unless Jeremy comes over." Jeremy was Jack's son.

Hope, said, "I'm going to watch what I watch and then I'm going to turn the TV off. It's ugly waking in the morning with the thing flickering. It feels debauched."

Jack said, "I'm not going to order books from Amazon till I've read the ones on my shelves."

Hope said, "I'm going to hang up my clothes even when nobody is coming over. Nora is very severe with me." Nora was Hope's daughter.

The wine arrived. Jack did the label-checking, cork-sniffing, tasting and nodding. The salad came. Hope helped their two plates.

Jack indicated Hope's hair, which she had done in an upsweep. "Very fetching," he commented.

"Thank you. Here's an old resolution: going to learn French. What was the name of my teacher when we got back from Paris? I once counted eleven years of school French and it was you who had to do the talking."

Jack said, "I want to learn how to pray."

Hope looked across the table to see if he was being cute. Jack was concentrated on folding the whole piece of lettuce on his fork into his mouth.

Hope said, "I'll never understand the theory of not cutting it into bite sizes."

The onion soup came, the cassoulet came. Jack asked Hope if she would like to go back.

"Back? Back to Paris!" Jack and Hope had lived together before marrying two other people. Jack subsequently divorced his wife, who had subsequently died. Hope was widowed.

"To Paris. To Aix," said Jack.

"Something I've been meaning to ask you," Hope said. "Were you and I ever in this garden together? Did we walk under century-old trees? Did we lie in the grass and look up into tree crowns in France, or in England? Was it an old, old English garden? Is this a garden in a book?"

"What's to stop us?" Jack said.

There were a lot of reasons, of course, that stopped them from going back. Two of the littlest were this moment flattening their noses against the outside of the restaurant window. Ten-year-old Benjamin stuck his thumbs in his ears and wiggled his fingers at his grandfather. Hope made as if to catch her granddaughter's hand through the glass. Little Miranda laughed. "I'm just going to the bathroom," Hope mouthed to her daughter, Nora, out on the sidewalk.

"*What?*" Nora mouthed back, her face sharpened with irritation. "She knows I can't understand her through the window," Nora said to Jack's son,

Jeremy, and Julie, the baby in the stroller, started screeching. Jeremy said, "You stay with the kids. I'll go in and get him and see what she wants."

Jeremy walked into the restaurant, passing Jack and Hope on his way to the corner where, an hour ago, he had folded up his father's wheelchair. Hope stood up, came around the table, kissed Jack and got kissed goodbye.

"On the double, Dad!" Jeremy said, "I need to get back to the office."

"I'll call you," Jack said to Hope. "We'll have lunch."

Hope mouthed to her daughter through the window. "Julie, shut up, *please*! Mom, *WHAT?*"

Hope pointed in the direction of the ladies' room. Nora signalled, "You need me to go with you?"

Hope shook her head, no. One of the reasons for the Café Provence was that its bathrooms were on the street floor, not down a long stair in the basement.

Gathering coat and bag, Hope opened the door into the ladies' room and saw, in the mirror behind the basins, that her hair was coming out of its pins. She took the pins out and stood gazing at the crone with the grey, shoulder-length hair girlishly loosened. Hope saw what Diane Arbus might have seen. She gazed, appalled, and being appalled pricked her interest. "I've got an agenda: the Arbus factor in old age," Hope looked forward to saying to Jack the next time it would be convenient for Jeremy and Nora to arrange lunch for them at the Café Provence.

5

Soft Sculpture

"My birthday party was in March," Ilka told Bridget. The two old friends were walking on Riverside Drive at the turn of the season when you learn all over again that 49 degrees requires more than a jacket. Ilka said "And I got what seemed an inspired present, a little ... a ... a ... what do you call the animal with the exoskeleton ... a ...?" Ilka frowned, impatient and irritated at ... at what was not, at that moment, available to her. "Bridget," she said, "what's the obvious – what is the first animal you think of that carries its roof, so conveniently attached, on its own back...?"

"A tortoise," said Bridget.

"A little tortoise," Ilka said. *"Eine Kleine Schildkröte.* The *Kröterl.* That was the week of the Hitler take-over."

Bridget stopped and turned to look at her friend, who said, "No way am I going to remember which of the six or seven little girls had brought what turned out to be an embarrassment. That thing sat and didn't *do* anything. Just sat there. We shoved it, we pushed, we poked, we nudged. It withdrew its head under its roof and would not and would not move. My mother to the rescue. Mutti took all the children into the bathroom. You have to understand that this is a bathroom in Vienna and it's the thirties. Mutti had to go find the matches and light the wall-mounted gas heater and warm two inches of water to cover the bottom of the tub, and she put in the *Kröterl* which began immediately to march, and it marched round and round the bathtub at the speed of an Olympic footrace.

"Next day the three brownshirts walked in and gave us twenty-four hours to be out of our apartment." If Ilka frowned, it was to find herself, still and again, rehearsing her ur-story.

When the ready tears that strangled Bridget's throat allowed her to speak, she asked, "Where could you go?"

Ilka said, "They took me to Edith's, a school friend. Mutti and Vati found beds with ... people."

Bridget was a writer with an indigestible Irish past of her own. Now she kept walking, alert to a fertile convergence in her understanding of the raw chill of a March day and of the word – the meaning of "apartment": having to leave where one was able to be apart; of being without – that is "outside" one's own walls, and without a roof. To have no roof.

"And the tortoise?" Bridget asked Ilka. "You took it with you?"

Ilka thought and she said, "I look back and I don't see ... the *Kröterl* didn't come with me to Edith's."

Bridget said, "But you remember leaving, walking out the door of your apartment? Did your mother take it? Your father?"

"What I remember", Ilka said, "is the bathroom in our old apartment, mornings, my father

45

sharpening his straight razor on the leather strop attached ... was it to the doorknob? Sounds like Bluebeard – poor Vati! And my recurring mishaps because I did not like to go into the bathroom after dark. Vati's terry-cloth robe, which hung on top of my mutti's robe behind the bathroom door, had a way of putting a ghostly sleeve on my shoulder."

Bridget, who tended to invoke Henry James, remembered James remembering a lady across the dinner table at one of those Victorian country weekends. Her account of a dowager's unwillingness to vacate her family home had given him the germ of an idea which, if the old gossip would stop with the unusable detail – "the muddle of reality", James called it – could be shaping what was to become his next novel.

"Before Hitler," Ilka was saying, "we used to summer in the mountains. I keep wanting to turn and ask my mother about the consignment of *Enzian* – the gentian that followed us home – an alpine bluebell that grows from the ground without a stem. Who sent such a mass of these bluest-blue flowers that the only place large enough was the bathtub?"

"Dead or alive," Bridget said with a degree of anxiety, "the tortoise must have gone somewhere."

"When my kids were little," Ilka said, "I got them a stuffed toy, a soft sculpture, a green *Kröterl*. The *-erl* ending is the Viennese diminutive; in German it would have been a *Krötchen*. It must still be somewhere around the apartment. It was a handpuppet. You could put your hand inside and make it draw its head back in under its stuffed cotton roof."

"And now," Bridget said, "MyKroeterl38@ usa.com is your email. It's how I write to you."

"Yes," Ilka said. "Now that's my address."

6

Mother Lear

When Bessie said, "Don't we think of King Lear of Act One, before he goes officially crazy, as a silly old man?" the friends around the ladies' lunch table listened up. "But then," continued Bessie, "we get old and we have daughters. Yesterday, Eve and Jenny turned up in Old Rockingham to say goodbye..."

"Where are they going?" asked Farah.

"... Came to say goodbye," went on Bessie, "at a time when Colin is going to need more and more of me."

"But they're not Colin's, they're Eli's children, aren't they?" Farah asked her.

"Yes. They plan to spend a week with their father in London. Then they're off for a month – an open-ended month, maybe longer, in Spain, Italy..."

"Aren't you thrilled for them?" Farah prompted her.

"Well, there's the rub," Bessie said. "What poor old Lear requires are the over-the-top demonstrations of love from his grown-up daughters when the reasonable attachment of his true and dutiful child drives him berserk."

Lotte said, "Why, for god's sake, should your children spend goodness knows how many of their young years sitting at home watching their step-father?"

"Why, Lotte," said Bessie, "are you explaining to me what I thought I was explaining to you. That's what I'm saying. Of course it's nonsense but, but... but then why does their leaving leave me feeling like the motherless child?"

"Because you had hoped to put yourself into their *kind nursery?*" Farah quoted.

"Heck, no! God no!" Bessie said, "But, but..."

Bridget, the writer in the group, said, "You would make a better protagonist of your story if you didn't diagnose the Mother Lear aspect up front. There's nowhere for the plot to develop."

"Assign me my role," laughed Bessie. "I'll see if I can play it."

"Could you perhaps feel *how sharper than a serpent's tooth it is to have thankless daughters*, and might you curse both of them with barren wombs?"

Lotte said, "Hasn't even occurred to me to curse my Samson when he offers to find me a twenty-four-hour home aide."

"Boring of us," Bessie said. "Our lot makes decent protagonists; we don't do the tragic."

Ruth, the retired lawyer and old militant, said, "You might try doing poor Lear turned lefty: *Expose yourself to feel what wretches feel* – how does it go? – *and shake the superflux to them. And show the Heavens more just.*"

"Yes, well," Bessie said, "except that we come indoors out of the rain and sit around the table diagnosing our sorrows like commonsensical old women. Our children would not believe how calmly we look around the table wondering which one of us will be next."

7

Around the Corner
You Can't See Around

Ladies' lunch over and talk for the moment exhausted, we continued around the table by the window that overlooked the Hudson River, sipped the wine, poured ourselves another glass. It was here that Bridget asked what everybody thought about this idea of 'finding oneself'. "Is there a character in Homer, in Shakespeare, in the Bible who thinks to ask 'Who am I?'"

"Except for King Lear, who asks, 'Who is it that can tell me who I am?'" said Farah, and the conversation was off again. She said, "Don't you love the question 'Who does he think he is?' or 'Who do you think you are?' followed by a rhetorical exclamation point?"

Hope's chair faced east. She had been watching the people on the neighbouring rooftop, and she said, "They're having a party and they didn't invite me!"

"Do you know those people?" Ruth asked Hope.

"No," Hope said.

Ilka said her search began with her grandmother Ilonka, the one she was named for. "She died before I was born, but I've seen an old sepia photograph –actually two photographs taken from two positions through an open door into her bedroom. Great Aunt Mali used to let me play with – what did they call it? – the stereopticon, Sunday afternoons when my mother's cousins used to get together in her apartment just outside Vienna – I don't think I remember my father being there. Tante Mali was immensely fat and old, with a sweet, lovely face. She and the little Onkel Max ended up in Mauthausen.

The magic of the stereopticon made the flower in the water glass, made the glass three-dimensional and more real than the sepia grandmother sitting up in her crocheted bedjacket."

Lotte frowned irritably when she said, "I will never understand why something made to look three-dimensional or virtual excites us more than the real thing in front of our noses..."

"Mimesis," Farah said. "Is it Aristotle or is it me who said we like a likeness, in which, I guess, we search for ourselves?"

Ilka was following her own thought: "The room is lighted from the left, so there must be a window in the corner that one can't see around? Secrets of the sepia bedroom. Someone had picked that flower and put water into the water glass; someone had set the glass on the bedside table..."

"That's what I mean!" Lotte said irritably. "What does it tell us about who we are, that we are tenderly intrigued by an imaginary person walking through an old photograph but couldn't care less about the neighbour passing our window at this very moment?"

"My mother found the old ice skates," continued Ilka. "The grandmother in the bedjacket ice-skating blew my mind. I mean, when were skates even invented?"

Ruth consulted her smartphone. She said, "In 3000 BC."

"Look!" Hope said. "Look! The people on the roof! They're bringing out the cake. It's a birthday party."

"Birthdays," Bessie said. "People talk of having missed their own, or their kid's birthday, or graduation. Tell me one thing that ever signified at a birthday party, a graduation, at Thanksgiving, a Seder, a wedding even..."

"Or funeral," said Farah.

Ruth said, "Next ladies' lunch will be at my place. The agenda: tell some one thing that has thrown light on 'Who You Are'."

At Ruth's table, next ladies' lunch, I read them what I had written about the morning I woke in my first English foster home:

"There, on a chest of drawers, was the suit-case my mother had packed for me. I lay in a strange bed and wondered what I was supposed to do. Presently I got up, I dressed slowly, and opened the door to the hallway. Where were all the people? The previous night there had been an old woman in a fur coat and her daughter who had fetched me from the station and brought me to this house where all the lights were on in all the rooms and a lot of smiling people looking at me. A maidservant in a long white apron had taken me upstairs to the bathroom and ran a bath. I understood she meant me to get in, but I was ashamed and would not undress, and in the morning I could not remember having been brought up to this bedroom. I stepped out into the hallway and listened to the silence. A door stood ajar. I looked inside and saw a dressing table. There were photographs stuck into the frame of the mirror which reflected a brush, a comb and a pincushion in the shape of a heart. I gave the door what

I told myself might have been an accidental push. It revealed the corner of somebody's bed covered with a shiny green counterpane. I knew I must not walk into other people's bedrooms – should not be looking in. Was I allowed – was I meant to use these stairs? I crept down to the next floor. There were a number of doors, but all of them were shut."

"Bedrooms," said Bessie. "It was Robbe-Grillet, if you please, showed us that before we give ourselves account of the colour of the wall or form a relation with this or that piece of furniture we are part of that earliest geography. Try it! Imagine yourself into bed in your first bedroom; notice that you know the direction your feet are pointing; and you remember the location of the door in relation to the window..."

"And you define yourself as who inhabited that first bedroom?" Ruth asked her.

"Why do I have to define myself?" asked Bessie.

I said, "Well, I am the refugee who keeps telling the old story."

"And I", Hope said, "am the uninvited."

"But you're not," said Lotte. "You are at the ladies' lunch. Why am I the one the person at the party who argues with everything anybody says?"

"And I", said Farah, "the one who brings up the things nobody is interested in thinking about?"

"And you?" Ruth said to Bridget. "It's you who got us asking ourselves who we are. What do you say?"

"That there is no 'Who'," Bridget said. "I think it's a silly question."

8

Ladies' Lunch

It matters that Lotte's apartment is commodious. Lotte liked to boast that she lies in her bed and looks past the two closest water towers, past the architectural follies and oddities few people notice on Manhattan's rooftops, and sees all the way to the Empire State Building.

On the velvet sofa in Lotte's living room, from which one can observe the Hudson River traffic as far as the George Washington Bridge, the caregiver sits and watches television.

"Get rid of her," says Lotte.

Samson drops his voice as if this might make his mother lower hers. "As soon as we find you a replacement."

"And I'll get rid of *her*," says Lotte.

Sam says, "We'll go on interviewing till we find you the right one."

"Who will let me eat bread and butter?"

"Mom," says Sam, "bread turns into sugar, as you know very well."

"And don't care," Lotte says.

"If she let you eat bread for breakfast, lunch and dinner, she'd get fired."

"Good," says Lotte.

"Sarah," Sam says to the caregiver, "I'll take my mother to her ladies' lunch if you'll pick her up at three thirty?"

"That OK with you?" Sarah asks Lotte.

"No," says Lotte.

Ruth said, "Remember how we said we are the people in the world to whom we tell things. And that's us. Something happens and I think, I'll tell the next ladies' lunch."

"True! It's true," said Ilka. "When I suddenly sat on my rear on the sidewalk outside my front door, I was looking forward to telling you."

Ilka had turned out to need a hip replacement. Dr Barson, the surgeon, was a furry man like a character in an Ed Koren cartoon but jollier. "From here on it's all good," he promised Ilka.

"I'm eighty-five years old," said Ilka.

Barson told her, "I'm on my way to the ninety-second birthday of a patient on whom I operated eleven years ago."

"And *I*", said Bessie, "told *you*, from my poor Colin's experience, that the recovery is not so much like Barson's cheery projection." These days it depended on the state of Colin's deteriorating health and mood whether Bessie was able to take the train in from Old Rockingham.

Today's lunch was at Bridget's table and she said, "My agenda: 'How to Prevent the Inevitable.' I mean any of the scenarios we would rather die than live in."

Farah, a retired doctor said, "The old problem of shuffling off this mortal coil."

"Of shuffling off," said Lotte.

"And it was you", Farah reminded Lotte, "who said you wanted to see it all, to see what would happen to the end."

"I wasn't counting", said Lotte, "on the twenty-four-hour caregiver or the heart-healthy diet. You doctors need to do a study of the correlation between salt-free food and depression."

"Your Sarah seems pleasant enough," said Ruth. "What's wrong with her?"

"That she's in my living room", said Lotte, "watching television; that she's in my kitchen eating her lunch which she does standing up; that she sleeps in my spare room and is in my bathroom whenever I want to go in."

"What, at this point, do you need her to do for you? Do you need a caregiver to help you dress?"

"No," said Lotte.

"You need a caregiver to help you shower?"

"No," said Lotte.

"Get your meals?"

"God, NO!" said Lotte.

"So what do you need help with?"

"The caregiver," said Lotte.

"Go away," she said to Sarah who had come to take her home. The four women's mouths dropped to see their friend raise her arm and strike the empty air.

They were of an age when they worried if one of them did not answer her telephone.

Bessie, Lotte's oldest friend, had known Samson since he was a young child – a baby. She called him from Connecticut. "Why doesn't the caregiver pick up Lotte's phone?"

"The caregiver's gone. There was just too much abuse."

"You're kidding me? What! That nice Sarah? You're talking elder abuse?"

"Caregiver abuse," Sam said.

"Like what!"

"Like Mom would change the channel Sarah was watching on the TV. Like coming into the kitchen and packing away the food Sarah was preparing for her lunch. And turning the light on in the room where Sarah slept. It's getting bizarre. Anyway. I'm here waiting with her for the new woman."

Bridget, who still spent her mornings at her computer, writing, went up to see Lotte.

Bridget, Lotte and Shareen, the new caregiver, sat looking out on Riverside Drive.

Lotte said, "Shareen drives her car in from New Jersey. Shareen has a five-year-old who brushes his own teeth. Shareen has told him if he doesn't brush, a roach will grow in his mouth."

Bessie phoned Lotte from Connecticut. "How is the new caregiver?"

"Intrusive," said Lotte.

When Farah called Lotte, it was Sam who picked up the phone. "Shareen is gone. Mom locked her – I can't make out if it was into or out of the bathroom, but it wasn't that. Shareen did not want to have to manhandle Mom to stop her eating sugar by the spoonful. It's getting out of hand."

"Your mother is angry," said Farah. "Imagine making your own decisions your life long and now there's someone telling you what you can eat and when to shower and what to wear."

"Because her own decisions are no longer tenable," said Sam. "Greg is coming in from Chicago." Gregor was Lotte's younger son. "We're going to check out this nice assisted living home. It sounds really nice. Upscale."

"Sam! You're moving Lotte out of her apartment!"

"To a nice home in the country."

"A home in the country. You discussed this move with Lotte?"

"Yes."

"And she has agreed?"

"Well, yes, she has. In a way. She said next year, maybe. Listen," Sam said, "Mom cannot deal with the round-the-clock caregivers. And believe me that she does not, does NOT, want to move in with me and Diana."

Bridget phoned Sam. "What about this place you want to move Lotte into?"

"Called 'Green Trees' in the Hudson Valley. My brother will help me move Mom and move the stuff she is fond of – the famous velvet sofa."

"She'll have an apartment of her own?"

"A bedsitter, neat, convenient with her own bathroom and a breakfast nook."

"A breakfast nook," said Bridget. "What's outside the window?"

"The Hudson River view, unfortunately, is on the other side of the building. Trees. There's a small parking lot and lots of green. Listen. I know Mom would prefer Manhattan, which would have been a hell of a lot more convenient for Diana and me to visit her, but who can afford something nice in the city?"

Bridget said, "It's that none of *us* drives these days. How are *we* going to visit Lotte?"

"One of the advantages is that there will always be people around."

"People Lotte can talk to?"

Sam said, "I have never been in a situation where there hasn't been somebody conversable."

"Haven't you?" said Bridget.

"And she will be fed three proper meals, willy-nilly."

God. Poor Lotte, thought Bridget. *And poor Sam.* "I know you're not a happy camper," she said, and she wondered where that phrase came from.

Ruth, the old activist, said: "I have an idea. Let me talk to Samson."

"Have you closed with the Hudson Valley place?" she asked him.

"Greg and I are going up on Thursday."

Ruth said, "Can you give us a couple of days to figure something out?"

"Believe me there is nothing to... Yes. OK. But I need to move her and her stuff before Greg has to get back to Chicago."

Ruth said, "Could Lotte live alone if...?"

"Absolutely not."

"Sam, wait. Listen. Could Lotte live alone if the four of us – the three of us if Bessie can't come in – take turns checking in on Lotte, see what she needs and if anything was wrong..."

"Mom would put sugar on her bread and butter."

"Sounds delicious," said Ruth.

"She would never change her clothes."

"Probably not."

"She would have one shower a week. She would not shower."

"Sam! So *what!*"

"Not on my watch," Sam said. "Things need to be done right."

"No, they don't. Why do they need to be right?"

"When Mom messed up her medicines, Greg and I had to rush her to Emergency. She might have died."

"Yes, she might. Your mother might have died in her own bed, in sight of the Empire State Building and the George Washington Bridge. No, but Sam, we will go up, we will keep an eye on her. Let's try it – a couple of days."

"And what if she falls again?"

"She falls! Sam, I'll sleep over there tonight."

Ruth slept over at Lotte's and Lotte fell down going from her bed to the bathroom. Ruth called Sam, and Sam and Gregor came and took Lotte to Emergency.

Samson and Gregor moved their mother, the sofa and what, out of Lotte's ample apartment, could be made to fit into the bedsitter in the Hudson Valley, and Greg flew back to Chicago.

The next ladies' lunch met at Farah's table; the agenda was Farah's plan to rescue Lotte.

They brought each other up to date.

Lotte had phoned Farah from Green Trees. "I didn't recognise her voice. I mean, I knew it was Lotte, but her voice sounded different, strangled, a new, strange voice."

"She is furious," Bessie said.

"I know that voice," said Bridget. "She called me. Lotte remembers me sitting with her and Shareen. She wants me to get Shareen's phone number. Shareen drives a car. Lotte wants Shareen to pick her up at Green Trees and drive her home to the apartment. Which is not going to happen."

Ruth said, "Lotte wants us – her and me – to rent a car together. I told her I haven't renewed my licence. I doubt if I could pass the eye test. Not a problem, Lotte said. *She* would drive."

"Does Lotte even have a licence?"

"Lotte hasn't driven in ten years."

Bessie told them that Sam had called her, fit to be tied. "Wanted to know if I had something to do with Lotte buying a car! *Buying* a car! Me? I have never actually bought a car in my life. It seems Lotte keeps calling the dealer to send her the keys. I called Lotte and I asked her, 'What's this about a car?' Lotte said, 'Down in the parking lot.' I asked her, 'What kind of a car is this!' She said, 'I'm waiting for the virtual keys.'"

Farah's plan: her eighteen-year-old grandson, Hami, would have his licence as soon as he passed his test. "He will drive us to Green Trees and we will bring Lotte home."

"Better be soon," said Bessie. "Sam is putting Lotte's apartment on the market."

"The test is next Monday."

But Hami failed his test and, as of this moment, Lotte is at Green Trees in the Hudson Valley.

Bridget phones Lotte. "How's it going?"

"Not good."

"How is the food?"

"Salt free."

"Judging from your voice you're getting a *little* bit used to being there, Lotte? Yes?"

"Can you come and get me and take me home?"

"Lotte, we just really wouldn't know how. For the moment, might it be a good idea to accommodate yourself?"

"Yes," says Lotte. "But I need to get back to my apartment."

"Is there anyone to talk to?"

"Yes. Alana. She sits next to me in the dining room. Alana has five grandchildren, the oldest nineteen, twins age thirteen, and a nine- and a five-year-old. Would you like me to tell you what their names are?"

"Not really."

Would you like me to tell you where each of them goes to school?"

"Lotte..."

"Minnie's grandson is called Joel. His best friend's name is Sam, like my Sam. Shall I tell you which colleges Sam and which colleges Joel are considering going to?"

"Lotte..."

"Minnie's sister's granddaughter Lucy", says Lotte, "is thinking of taking a gap year before she goes to Williams..."

"*Lotte*...!"

Lotte says, "Alana and Minnie are not the people to whom I tell that I have died. I thought a while before telling Sam but he was fine with it. He was really good."

"You mean that you *feel* as if..." Bridget hesitates between '... as if you have died' and '... as if you are dead.'"

"No," says Lotte, "I *am* dead. If I saw Dr Barson, or any doctor, they would look down my throat and see the four yellow spots dead people have. When you write the story, there's the question whether, now that I've died, I can die again, a second time, or is this what it's going to be from here on?"

"Lotte, you want me to write your story?"

"You've already written how I got rid of Sarah and Shareen," says Lotte, "and the roach growing in

Shareen's five-year-old's mouth, and Sam and Greg putting me out in the boonies."

"Lotte," says Bridget, "we're mobilising ourselves. We're trying to figure out how to come and visit you."

"Good! Oh, oh, good, good!" says Lotte. "Give me enough lead time so I can arrange a ladies' lunch in the Green Trees dining room and I will tell you how I lay down on my sofa – this was last Friday, just to take a nap, and woke up and knew that I was going to die, and I died."

Sam has taken time off to go up and visit his mother twice in the last month. He feels that she is settling in. "When she says that she has died, it means died to the old New York life in order to pass into the new life at Green Trees."

"Sam, you think that's what she means?" Ruth asks him.

"What else?"

Ruth says, "Lotte doesn't call us."

"I know," says Sam, "She doesn't call me and she doesn't return Diana's calls."

"She doesn't pick up her phone."

"I know," says Sam.

Bessie is pretty much stuck in Old Rockingham. Colin seems to be on the decline. Poor Bridget didn't make it to the last ladies' lunch because she had one of her frequent and debilitating headaches, but she wants to come along if Ruth and Farah figure out how to go and visit Lotte.

There was an idea to hitch a ride with Sam the last time he drove up to Green Trees, but it got screwed up because Lotte hadn't returned Farah's call. "And then I guess I forgot to call *her*," says Ruth. "In any case, there wouldn't have really been time to change my doctor's appointment."

Hami has got his permit and has driven his new little second-hand car to his first semester at Purchase.

Farah, Ruth and Bridget, if she can make it, still mean to figure out some way to go up and visit Lotte, maybe in spring, when the weather is nicer.

9

Sans Teeth, Sans Taste

Bessie had called to say she might not make it to ladies' lunch.

"Colin is worse?" Farah asked her. Bessie's friends had little use for the one husband still alive, a man of large property and the wrong politics, but on the phone that morning Farah and Bessie had cried together about the unbearable fact of his suffering.

But then Bessie had come, had come early. "Poor old Farah!" she said. "You retired from doctoring, but we're still keeping after you! Whoever else is there? Farah! Is there a way out?"

"Ah," Farah said, "Our coming hither is hard, but getting out of here is harder."

"Is there a way?"

"Does Colin say...?"

"Never made a living will, but what he wants is not to have what is unbearable."

Farah reached into the drawer beside her and took out the End of Life file. "I happened to be looking through this and if you ask me, I will tell you what there is to know. But, Bessie, it is purposely not made easy ... One can take a trip to Switzerland where it's legal, and expensive; one can move to New Jersey, but you have to prove you have only six months to live. Or you can stop eating and drinking..."

Here's where the bell rang and Bessie said, "Farah, I don't want to dump on everybody until it can't be helped."

"I know, I know," Farah said. "Yes, I know," and then Ruth walked in, and Ilka, and Bridget, who said, "Guys, this is five years to the day of Lotte's birthday when she reminded us that she was crossing into her nineties from where she promised to send the rest of us regular reports."

"And you, Bessie, hid your eyes behind your hand and said, 'I don't know how you can you talk like this in public.'"

They laughed; they were quiet a long moment. They had watched their witty friend turn into the angry old person who abused her aides, irrationally – or was it rational to fight the two sons who put her into a well-run assisted living in the boonies from where – quite potty by this time – Lotte had never stopped plotting to drive herself home. And then she died.

When all were seated and served, Farah said, "May I remind us of the twenty-minute rule: that's how long we get to talk aches, pains, meds, etc. Then we move onto our agenda. Do let us have an agenda."

Ruth said, "Look! Lost a front tooth, and the bottom ones rattle."

Ilka said, "I thought I was all fixed when I came home from my left hip replacement. It didn't occur to me that I had a right knee and it was going to need surgery."

Bridget said, "I need my head replaced. I was doing a reading and there came the moment I kept reading without knowing what my story was about."

Ruth said, "It might be the teeth, but I have stopped eating. It's hard to shop for food that you can't imagine putting in your mouth and chewing."

Farah said, "I used to send my patients to a good nutritionist. Remind me, Ruth, before you leave, and I'll give you Johanna's number." And then she said, "My ophthalmologist tells me I am losing my vision."

"Losing?" Bessie said, "How do you mean *losing*? You can see to read."

"You can write," Bridget said.

Ilka said, "You see us, Farah. What do you see when you look at us?"

"I can read, I can write, and I see you a little less well every day," said Farah, but Ilka said, "You don't mean that you can see less today than you saw yesterday?"

That was what Farah meant. She could tell that her friends' anxiety meant her to not mean what they wanted not to know. It was Farah's educated understanding of the probability, say the possibility, that she was going blind that had sent her to her End of Life file, while she could still see to make the arrangements; to prepare her daughters, whose agreement and assistance she would need to stop eating. She felt sorry for them, sorry, in Bessie's words, to have dumped this on her friends

She slipped the file into the drawer and said, "Twenty minutes is up. What's our agenda?"

Farah remembered to give Ruth the nutritionist's number. "Call her. She's good. Next lunch at your place?"

When she had closed the door behind them, Farah surprised herself by dialling Johanna. "It's Farah. Yes! Long time. How I am? 'Well enough' is my all-purpose answer, except I have zero appetite. Any ideas?"

Other Stories

Dandelion

That Henry James, when he got old, rewrote his early work was my excuse for revisiting, at ninety, a story I had written in my twenties. I was ten years old when I had to leave Austria, so the day with my father in the Alps must have taken place on our last family holiday, the previous August.

I wished Mutti were coming, but she had woken with one of her migraines. I stood outside the hotel, in the grass, getting my shoes wet with dew, waiting and wanting for nothing. "Light tinkled among the trees," and the "grasses gleamed sword-like," says my story. Curious how our language asks for similes.

What is something *like*? The sky was "like liquid light," I wrote. "Liquid" is close, but it's not quite the right word. "The mountain's back looked like something sculpted; one had the feel of the distant footpath in the fingertips. Between the mountain and myself, the land cupped downward, containing light like a mist". How was it "like a mist," the essence of which is to obscure? I remember it as a white, chilly presence. A dog barked and barked and barked and the purity of the air carried the sound to where I stood waiting.

On the road at the end of the hotel gardens, a group of silent walkers passed at the steady pace of those who have a day's march ahead of them, young people. I followed them with my eyes. This was the moment that the sun crested the mountain – a sudden unobstructed fire. It outlined the young people's backs with a faintly furred halo, while here, in the garden, it caught the head of a silver dandelion, fiercely, tenderly transfigured into light. I experienced a bliss of thought, new and inevitable, and I said, "*Lieber Gott*, if I ever ask you for anything, you don't even have to listen, because nothing is necessary except this." I knew that was right because of my vast happiness, and then my father called me and we walked out of the garden and started up the road.

My *vati* was a tall man in excellent spirits. In August, the Viennese banks closed. In the mountains, my father wore knickerbockers and an Alpine hat with a feather. In his pocket he had a book in which to look up the names of the wayside flowers, trees and birds. As we climbed, he pointed through the pines to the village further and further away below us. Vati's plan was to reach the *Alm* by noon and take our lunch in the *Alm* hut. Did I know, he asked me, what an *Alm* was? It was a meadow high in the mountains where the cowherd brought all the cows from the valley to spend the summer eating the healthful upper grass, but I was being the world-famous ice-skating star Lucinda in her velvet dress with a skirt that swirled when I did my world-famous pirouette, and I couldn't listen to what my father was explaining.

Oh, but the sky was blue! It is bluest when you lie on your side and look through the grasses that grow by your cheek. I watched a spider climb a stalk that bent under its weight.

I sat up. People were coming along the path, two men – young men walking together, one talking, using his hands. The other, who walked with his eyes to the ground, brought up his head and said something that made the first one shout with laughter. I watched them. They slowed their steps to look back at the people coming behind them. One of the girls called gaily, and the two groups joined. That was what I wanted to do when I got older – walk with friends, talking together and laughing.

I looked after them with a suddenly sharpened interest. "You know something? Vati? I think those are the people I saw on the road this morning, when I was waiting for you. Vati, do you think they are the same people?"

Vati was asleep. It was rare, it was awesome, to see a sleeping grown-up. His two shoes pointed skyward. Where his trouser leg folded back it exposed a piece of leg above the sock. I averted my eyes.

We resumed our ascent and it was hot and grew hotter. The climb became harder and steeper, until

I thought I could not lift my foot to take the next step, and the next, and the next for the several hours it took us to reach the top.

It was many years later, lying in the semi-dark and stillness, cleaned up and dry, after birthing my baby, my first – I could see where she lay wrapped, not crying, and everything was well – that I remembered sitting at long last, after climbing beyond my strength, under a tree in the shade, breathing in and out.

You know you have reached the top of the mountain when you are looking at a new world, the existence of which, a moment ago, you could not have suspected, ranges upon ranges paling into the blue distance, and here a peak rising and a second and a third, the relation in which they stand to one another becoming familiar under the blue sky. On the green expanse the cows graze, or move a step from here to there. When they lower their slow heads to chew the grass, the bells around their necks softly jingle.

My young folk sat at a long trestle table in the Alm hut. The cowherd, who sat with them, had a pipe between his teeth. The rumble of his voice, interrupted by the young people's chatter and laughter, made its way to the table where my Vati and I were having our *Mittagessen*. It was a meal that I still think about and have not been able to reproduce: *Kaiserschmarrn* (the Emperor's Pancake) served with blueberries. Alpine blueberries grow low to the ground and are both sweeter and sharper than the fruit you know. And a glass of fresh cow's milk.

I ate and watched. The girls were pretty and talked; the boys were tall and thin. I could see their knees. I loved how they clapped one another on the back and put pepper in one another's soup and liked one another. I wanted to talk about them and I asked Vati who they were and where they were going, but he quieted me with a gesture. Vati, a city man, took an interest in the Alpine type and wanted to listen to what the cowherd was saying.

There was a general movement – the meal was breaking up. The young people gathered themselves. Vati and I followed them out of the cool dark of the hut into the sheer heat of midday. One

of the boys, whose yellow hair jutted over his fore-
head, stood by the door adjusting the straps of his
rucksack. Vati also took an interest in young people
and questioned the boy about his party and their
plans. Leaning against my father's leg, I listened to
the boy's companionable answers and felt that life
could offer no better happiness. Vati was reminded
of his own young touring days and launched upon
an anecdote. It was hot. I squeezed my eyes against
the fierce brightness in which the blond boy's head
expanded and contracted among the little waves
of heat. Vati's voice proceeded upon the air, wanting to convey an idea of the exact conical rock
formation that had been attempted. He described
the attempt, and the failure that he, Vati, had
predicted. I watched the boy's hands play nervously
with the ends of his straps and said, "Vati!", saw the
boy's eyes steal to where his companions waited a
little way along the path, and said, "Vati, let's *go!*"
Vati was recounting the witty remark made by
himself in connection with said attempt and failure, laughing largely, recalling the occasion. The
blond boy cackled foolishly. I saw the boy looking

foolish and tugged on Vati's sleeve. *"Let's go!"* The boy excused himself, had his hand wrung long and heartily, dived for his freedom, and was received with laughter and a round of applause.

My face burned and I did not turn to look after the young people. They were going further on and Vati and I started on our homeward journey.

The intensity of the midday light had burned the colour out of things and deadened them. I was angry with the boy who had not wanted to hear Vati's story and had wanted to get away from Vati. I hated the young people who had clapped their hands and had laughed. My father was walking along in a flow of spirits, and I was sorry for him because I had not cared to listen to the things he wanted to tell me. I resented and disliked this bad feeling, which would not let me be comfortable and be Lucinda the world-famous skating star.

And I began to grizzle. I was tired, I said. There was a stone in my shoe and I didn't feel like carrying my cardigan. Vati stopped his yodelling and looked at me. There was no stone. Vati put the cardigan in his backpack. I rubbed my right temple with the back of my right hand and said I wanted to go home. We were *going* home, Vati said, we were on our way home, but I meant home *now.* Vati said, "We'll be home soon, we're almost home, in a couple of hours." He offered to tell me the story of Rikki-Tikki-Tavi, and the fight between the mongoose and the snake, but he had told it to me before. "How about an ice cream when we get home?" I understood that my father did not know what to do with me when I was like this, and I was afraid. I knew that this was God's awe-full answer, for hadn't I told him in the morning, "If I ever ask you for anything, you don't have to listen, because nothing is necessary except *this.*"

The sun was gone, all light absorbed by the ring of mountains that stood around us, soft and velvet purple, without the play of colour or movement save for our panicked descent. My father had hold of my wrist and hurried me along so that the stones rolled underfoot.

Making Good

Rabbi Rosen liked circles. They rearranged their chairs and Gretel volunteered to go first: "I am Gretel Mindel. You are Margot Groszbart. You are Rabbi Rosen..."

The rabbi said, "How would you all feel about just: Gretel, Margot and Sam? Hard enough to remember twenty new first names, no?"

Gretel started over. "I am Gretel, you are Margot, Rabbi Sam, Bob and Ruth. Erich. Steffi. And you are...?"

"Konrad Hohenstauf," murmured the eldest of the ten Viennese visitors – elegant, fragile, a little tremulous like a man after a heavy illness. He had a high, narrow nose – an alp of a nose, thought Margot Groszbart, who was one of the ten Viennese-born New Yorkers. Margot liked to say the only thing she missed was the mountains.

Konrad Hohenstauf's papery brown lips parted as if reluctantly: "Gretel. Margot. Rabbi Sam. Bob and Ruth. Erich. Steffi . Father Sebastian. And you?" He looked past – not at – Shoshannah Goldberg, who was hard to look at. If looking at Shoshannah was hard, it was impossible to not look and try to figure out what was wrong – beside the inward-turning left eye, the abbreviated left leg and frozen shoulder – with the way that she was held together.

Shoshannah Goldberg forgot the name of the forgettable Erich Radezki, and Erich got as far as Fritz Cohn with the Kaiser Franz Joseph moustache. Gretel Mindel was the first to remember all the names and close the circle.

Rabbi Sam invited everybody's input. "Questions? Any suggestions anybody would like to share?"

"Yes, I," said the responsive Gretel Mindel. "This morning I walked into this room and was surprised with myself that I believed that all you..." and Gretel Mindel did not, of course, say "all you Jews". She said, "that all you in New York must know each other. I surprised myself that I believed this." Gretel appeared to be addressing herself to Margot Groszbart. During their first American breakfast of sugared doughnuts and bad coffee, Gretel had failed to get close enough to talk to the elderly pianist whom she had once seen from the back of a Vienna concert hall. From across the room in New York, Margot Groszbart looked to have retained a lot of black in her hair. Her eyes had a snap; they lighted briefly and without particularity on Gretel Mindel before continuing to rove the room. Gretel understood that she had made no impression on the elderly Jewish musician.

Margot Groszbart had surprised herself too. After not responding to Rabbi Rosen's repeated and particular invitation that she join his Bridge Building Workshop, she found herself on the phone postponing a visit to her daughter in Los Angeles. Rachel said, "I thought you said Rabbi Rosen wasn't your cup of tea." "I know, but it's interesting – ten of us stuck in a room with ten of them. *Unlike* your Brooklyn mother-in-law, I don't walk around in a state of chronic Holocaust anger." "Why don't you?" asked Rachel. "Don't know," said her mother. "Don't have the chronic anger gene like your dear *mother-in-law*." A tender soul, Rachel refrained from questioning her mother's chronic anger toward her mother-in-law and only said, "So then come the week after and tell us how it went."

And so here, at eight o'clock on this particular Monday morning, Margot Groszbart sat on a bottom-chilling metal folding chair in the windowless basement meeting room under Rabbi Samuel Rosen's reform synagogue. The upright in the corner had the jolly, debauched look of a bar-room piano. Here, for the next five days, she was going to sit building bridges with the children and children's children of the Hitler generation.

Rabbi Sam liked Gretel's input. "Isn't that what we have come together *for*? To tell each other – and ourselves – what we don't even know that we are thinking about each other?"

"What don't we know that we are thinking?" said Ruth Schapiro. Across her breakfast coffee, Margot Groszbart had come to feel as if she had always known this small old woman – neat ankles, nice blue suit, hair nicely kept, the kind of red that got redder with each passing year. Bob Schapiro looked at his wife and she said, "We know what we are thinking."

"And will you share it with us?" Rabbi Sam asked. Bob Schapiro looked at Rabbi Sam and his wife said, "The six million."

Konrad Hohenstauf looked at his shoes. He lifted pointed, tremulous fingers to cover his mouth, which must once more have parted because Father Sebastian Pechter seated on his right and Shoshannah Goldberg on his left heard him murmur, "What I have done. *Ach*, what I have done..."

To fill the resulting pause, Margot Groszbart said, "I have a question. How is it all of you speak such efficient English?" The Austrians demurred. "Well, you seem to get said what you want to say." Margot had given up the attempt to activate her rusty childhood German, first in conversation with the round-chinned, baby-cheeked Erich, then with the priest who had stood before her bent at the waist as if in a condition of bowing. Neither of the young men had been about to give up the opportunity to practise his English. Margot said, "Why could I never get my American daughter to learn any German?"

"Why do you want her to learn German?" asked Ruth Schapiro.

Rabbi Sam was master of his own Socratic method: When the input he had asked for turned the conversation off-plan, he knew an exercise to fetch it home. He asked them to go around the circle and free-associate with their given names, which they did until the boy appeared with a great cardboard box of Cokes and brown-paper bags of kosher lunches.

The circle is not a natural configuration for a roomful of strangers. The young Austrians – Erich, Steffi and Gretel – went out to discover the New York neighbourhood; Rabbi Sam had synagogue business and invited Father Sebastian to accompany him.

The others disposed themselves about the ugly room and avoided each other's eyes. The elderly people – Austrian and Jew – went for the chairs set out around a number of small tables at which the rabbi intended to break his bridge-builders into working units. At one of these tables Bob and Ruth Schapiro shared their lunch bags companionably, wordlessly, as Margot imagined them sharing a lifetime of breakfasts, lunches and suppers. Margot had been widowed for decades. At another table Konrad Hohenstauf supported his chin on the handle of his cane and seemed to sleep. Plump, pretty Jenny Birnbaum, the only bridge-builder born in the New World, had spread her coat on the floor, curled up, and really had fallen asleep. Fritz Cohn, the Jewish stage-Viennese, shirt-sleeved, beer-bellied, moustachioed, lit a pipe and walked to and fro.

The lifelong and daily discipline of the performer translated doing nothing into guilt. Margot had sacrificed a week's practice and ought to be making use of her time talking to someone. The unusually tall Austrian woman in the plum-coloured turban sat close enough for conversation, but her back was hunched and to the room. It had become oppressively hot. A midday lassitude fixed Margot onto her chair.

For the afternoon session Rabbi Sam had them go around the circle and speculate on the name they would have given themselves if they had been their own parents. Konrad Hohenstauf asked to be permitted to pass, and passed when, after supper, they had to complete the sentence "When I came into the room, I thought..." going anti-clockwise.

Tuesday morning the rabbi handed out blank sheets of paper and crayons, saying, "Don't think, draw."

Gretel Mindel followed Margot to one of the little tables. Gretel said, "I heard you play in the Akademie theatre. *Wunderbar.*"

People made a mistake thinking this a propitious opening for conversation. A decent "Well, thank you", returned the ball to the flatterer, who had nowhere to go with it except on and on. Margot gave Gretel Mindel her professional smile. Margot Groszbart saw the girl's eagerness. She did not return it.

These young Viennese knew how to dress. In black on black, with the hair left to look slept in, and not the least make-up to cover her rather sallow complexion, Gretel Mindel was, in her way, a beauty. While talking with the undersexed Erich and the overly correct Father Sebastian, Margot had felt a familiar chill, which she now experienced sitting across from Gretel Mindel. Margot took it for granted that *she* must be radiating towards the Austrians a – reciprocally alien – heat. She gave a laugh. The girl raised a hopeful face.

Margot said, "I'm looking forward to getting Rabbi Sam's goat."

"His goat, please?"

"I'm going to irritate Rabbi Sam by telling him my racial theory based on an incompatibility of body temperatures."

"It is a joke?" asked Gretel Mindel.

"Yes, yes," said Margot and had once more surprised herself: why make herself interesting to the Austrian girl? Margot presently said, "Asking me to draw something is like asking me to say something. My head goes empty."

"I know! I know!" cried the girl. "I know exactly what you mean! Mine also!" Gretel Mindel now searched her mind for some other human oddity that she and the elderly Jewish pianist might discover to have in common. Gretel asked Margot if she, on entering the room yesterday morning, had thought of the Viennese as a cohort. "Were you surprised we did not even all know each other's names?"

Margot considered and replied that that wasn't what she happened to have been thinking. "I was thinking how I never walk into a room full of new people without a drop of the heart: I look around and think, 'Is *this* really all that's available?' My folks as well as yours."

Gretel laughed nicely. "And I always look if there will be an available man."

The two women glanced across the room where the rosy Erich and the stylish Steffi sat on the floor side by side bent over their drawings. It reminded Margot and Gretel to take up their crayons.

"In my age group," Margot said, "there is Bob." Bob Schapiro was a heavy man in a brown suit. He wore a yarmulke.

Gretel said, "But not available."

"Well," said Margot, "there's always – what *is* the name of the fellow who did something but won't say what?"

"Konrad Hohenstauf," said Gretel. She drew silently awhile before she asked, "It is permitted to make jokes?"

Margot said, "Bob and Ruth probably think it's sacrilege, but I refuse to think of the Holocaust as a sacred event."

Gretel kept drawing.

Margot, who wasn't sure she agreed with her own logic, felt uncomfortable arguing it before the Austrian. She was drawing a train that started on the left edge of her paper and travelled off the right edge. She made a row of windows. She drew a face in each window.

Gretel said, "I have made – a Munch." In the foreground she had drawn the back view of a lollipop-shaped human form facing the back of another lollipop in the middle distance. She said, "But your heart does not drop at Rabbi Sam."

"It doesn't?" said Margot.

Both looked in the direction of a pleasant incongruity – the stout rabbi with the drama of his grizzled full beard, sitting cross-legged on the floor. His sad, hot eyes above their sacks of flesh were fixed on the paper before him: Rabbi Sam was drawing.

Gretel said, *"Der schaut so lieb aus.* I don't know how one says this in English."

Margot said, "Because it can't *be* said. English won't let someone 'look dear'. You can say someone has a look of sweetness, I guess."

"Oh, but I think that is what he has! You think he has it, don't you?" Gretel urged Margot.

"I don't expect the concept of the sixties rabbi is familiar to you?"

"I was born in 1964," said Gretel. It was the year of Margot's daughter's birth.

Margot said, "Somewhere under that mass of coats behind the piano there's got to be the guitar."

Gretel Mindel and Margot Groszbart took their lunch bags to the little green community garden across from the synagogue. It was a windy blue day, barely warm enough to sit. Gretel told Margot that her mother had taken her to the Akademie to hear Margot play. Margot ate her sandwich and tried to figure Gretel's mother's age and wondered what she might have been doing between 1938 and 1945. She did not ask Gretel. There exists a shyness – a species of embarrassment – between the party of the murderer and the party of the murdered.

"You played *Das Wohltemperierte Klavier*," said Gretel.

"So I did." Fellow bridge-builders passed on the sidewalk.

"Who is the woman in the turban?" asked Margot. "I don't think I've heard her voice."

"Peppi Huber. We think she doesn't speak English."

Margot asked Gretel where she had learned her English.

"I was six months at the University of Texas."

They waved to Konrad walking with his cane and Shoshannah limping beside him. Shoshannah waved back.

Margot said, "How old can Konrad have been in 1938?"

From a tooth-whitening ad in her dentist's office, Margot had learned that it takes fifteen distinct facial muscles to operate the human smile. These muscles must have frozen Gretel Mindel's jaw and welted the area about the mouth.

Gretel said, "My mother liked to tell that she was the youngest youth leader in her district. Here comes Rabbi Sam. We go back," and, deeply frowning, she asked Margot *why* she didn't like the rabbi.

"Oh, but I do! How can one not like Rabbi Sam? But I don't much care for exercises that force-feed intimacy and pressure-cook healing."

"Better than not cooking!" pleaded Gretel. "You and I are here talking."

Poor Gretel. Margot felt she was disappointing her.

In the afternoon session they went around the circle and explained their drawings to each other. There is always, everywhere, a little pool of talent and a larger lack of it. Bob Schapiro looked at his wife and said, "I don't draw." Across his paper he had written

"March 12 1938", the date of Hitler's annexation of Austria, in black capitals.

Konrad had removed the paper sleeve from a black crayon and rolled it, at side down, from the top to the bottom of his paper, the darkness that covered what it was that he had done.

Fritz Cohn had drawn an adorable pair of *Lederhosen*. He said, "You can take the Jew out of Vienna but you can't take Vienna out of the Jew."

"You can," said Ruth Schapiro. She had drawn a Mogen David on a blue-white-blue background.

Shoshannah's drawing depended entirely on explanation: "There was no khaki crayon, but this is supposed to be a soldier. I don't know how to draw a person kneeling, but he is kneeling down planting something. I think he maybe lost his company or went AWOL and got a job on this farm."

"Went AWOL from which army?" asked Ruth Schapiro.

Shoshannah didn't know. "Someone maybe stole his uniform jacket, or he bartered it."

"Is he an ally or a Nazi?"

"We couldn't tell. The white with the red is the bloody bandage round his head. In the background, these are supposed to be burned-out farms. These are puffs of smoke from guns. We didn't know if we were behind the front line or ahead, or if the war was over and they weren't telling us. Maybe they didn't know. They were marching us south as it turned out, and I remember this soldier kneeling, planting something. You see the row of green? Anyway. Sam said to draw something."

Bob Schapiro looked at Shoshannah. Ruth Schapiro said, "What has this to do with the murder of the six million?"

It was here that Margot peered around the room: some of the Austrians looked at their shoes; some looked straight before them. Konrad's fingers covered his mouth.

Shoshannah's drawing was destined to start a side discussion that lasted the four remaining days: Shoshannah held that a head wound is a head wound is a head wound, while Ruth argued that you have to know if it was the head of a soldier who had killed or a soldier who had liberated Jews.

Erich said, "My father died of a head wound in Russia," but he said it in German to Steffi, later, when they were walking back to the hotel.

Jenny Birnbaum had drawn three skeletons – her grandparents and a baby uncle on her mother's side.

The Austrians looked straight before them.

Margot's turn: "The faces in the windows of the train are the children leaving Vienna. These figures in the background are waving parents."

Gretel Mindel looked stricken. Margot saw it.

Margot went on: "It bothers me to this day that I couldn't make out my mother among the people milling on the platform. I can't tell you if it's once a year, or if it's once a month that I call up the scene and try to catch Mutti waving while the platform gets smaller and goes out of sight."

Ruth Schapiro asked Margot, "Did your parents get out?"

"No. When they invited me to play at the Akademie I went and looked in the Resistance Archive. They were numbers 987 and 988 out of 1,030 on a train leaving Vienna June 14 1942, original destination Izbica, detoured to Trawniki."

"Bob and I don't go to Vienna," said Ruth Schapiro.

The Austrians looked straight before them. Margot thought, "Where are they *supposed* to look? What do we want them to do with their eyes?"

Rabbi Sam went last. "A bridge," everybody said, "over a lot of water."

The evening produced the guitar. Rabbi Sam taught the Austrians to sing Hatikvah. They sang "*Ach, du lieber Augustin*."

Gretel said, "You don't sing?"

"I'm willing, but my mouth is not." Margot's mouth would not open to sing Hatikvah; it would not sing "Oh, say can you see..." It refused to sing anything communally, at anybody's command, even at the request of the infinitely well-intending Rabbi Samuel Rosen. From this Margot Groszbart chose to deduce that, if birth had made her an Aryan in Vienna in 1938, she would not have sung the *Horst Wessel Lied*, that she could not have been seduced to open her mouth and communally shout "*Heil Hitler*".

Wednesday, Margot told Gretel she was going to eat in and talk to people and found her path promptly blocked by the plum-coloured turban. "*Ich will dir etwas sagen.* I want to say something to you."

It is usually a mistake to sit down with a person one doesn't know, because it is so hard, afterwards, to think of a polite reason for getting up again. But Margot could think of no polite reason for not sitting down and followed the tall, purposeful back to one of the small tables. They sat down. The turban approached so close it blurred in Margot's vision. The woman spoke the so-familiar Viennese German: "There was no anti-Semitism in Vienna before Waldheim," she said. "This time it is the Jews' fault." Her eyes held Margot's eyes. She was waiting.

Margot said, "Is it possible that you don't recognise this old line?"

"I know. I do. But this time it is true." The turban waited intensely.

Margot said, "I can't have this argument with you," and, needing no excuse, got up and left the woman sitting. She saw the Schapiros by the coffee urn and walked over.

Ruth Schapiro said, "We heard you play. Bob, what was it we heard Margot Groszbart play? Wonderful."

Bob Schapiro said, "Wonderful."

"Thank you," said Margot. "I've been thinking about this not going back to Vienna. I think what I think is that *not* going back packs just about the wallop of sticking one's tongue out at hell's gate, no?"

"And we don't buy German-made," said Ruth Schapiro.

Margot told them of her encounter with the purple turban and Ruth said, "So? An anti-Semite. What else is new?"

Margot looked back at Peppi, who continued to sit where she had left her sitting. Her head appeared to be sinking in the direction of her lap. "What's new, maybe, is she's an *uncomfortable* anti-Semite. I think she was asking me to argue her out of it."

"An anti-Semite is an anti-Semite, period," said Ruth Schapiro.

"What made the two of you come to Rabbi Rosen's bridge-building?" Margot asked them.

"He begged us. He was afraid no Jews would come."

Margot carried her cup of coffee away and chatted awhile with young Steffi. Steffi's mother, it turned out, had gone to Margot's old district, *Volksschule*. Margot reported the Waldheim conversation to Steffi who looked disgusted and said, "*Die is Antisemit*. She's an anti-Semite."

Steffi wanted Margot to tell her all the anti-Semitic remarks she remembered from her school days and was disappointed when Margot couldn't recall any.

Wednesday afternoon the rabbi paired them off and sent them to the little tables to interview each other. Steffi and Bob Schapiro, Ruth and Father Sebastian, Shoshannah Goldberg and Konrad Hohenstauf. One had to wonder what language young Jenny Birnbaum and the plum-coloured turban were going to interview each other in, but the baby-cheeked Erich and the historically mustachioed Fritz might hit it off.

Gretel Mindel asked to go with Margot. A premature nostalgia made her bag the table at which they had drawn pictures together. Gretel was wanting to confess. Gretel's *mutti* had led a cadre to Poland, her job to establish the "Jew houses" in which the deportees could be held over till their transportation to the final destination. Gretel's mother would give a Polish farm family twenty-four hours to load what they could onto a wagon and get out of the area. Gretel's mother boasted of never once having had to use her whip.

Gretel asked about Margot's *mutti*. Margot experienced a substantial reluctance, but said, "OK. Here's something I remember: when I was a bad child and didn't put my toys in the toy chest, my *mutti* would be angry and not look at me and not talk to me. So long as my *mutti* was not talking or looking, it was impossible for me to play or do anything. I would walk round the apartment after her, saying, 'Sei *wieder gut! Sei wieder gut!*' – something else, by the way, that doesn't translate into English. You can't say, 'Be good again!'"

"'Don't be angry with me!'" suggested Gretel. "'Forgive me! Like me!'"

"Anyway," said Margot, "I kept walking behind her saying, '*Sei wieder gut!*' till she relented or more probably forgot."

Next morning they sat in a circle to report each other's stories. It was in the act of recounting Margot's little childhood memory that Gretel experienced that shock of recognising something one has merely known: the *mutti* whom the child Margot had followed round the apartment was the same *mutti* the child on the train had not seen waving, was the woman they had put on the train going east, who had never returned. Gretel's sentence was swallowed in a sob so that she could not immediately realign the muscles required to go on speaking.

Margot gave a straightforward account of Gretel's mother's Nazi career. "She never had to use her whip," she concluded.

Gretel said, "She did other things."

Shoshannah reported only her own faithful promise not to tell what it was Konrad had told her that he had done. She drew her chair up to his chair and, using her right hand to lift her inoperative left arm, laid the left hand on Konrad's wrist. "You were only eight years old!" she said to him.

Universally irritated – by the superior intensity of Gretel Mindel's emotion over her own ageing memory; by the mileage Konrad Hohenstauf was getting out of what he wasn't telling; by the hurt hunch of Peppi Huber's shoulders; the Schapiros' single incorruptible idea; and Sam Rosen's incorruptible goodwill – Margot walked out of that door and hailed a taxi. She opened the door into the calm of her handsome apartment, finished yesterday's soup, skimmed the *Times*, failed to reach her daughter on the telephone, and sat down for fifteen minutes at the piano before she got back into a taxi so as not to be late for the afternoon session.

Morning and noon of their last day. Gretel, Steffi and Erich took Margot to lunch in the little corner restaurant they had discovered. When the conversation relaxed into German they forgot that she wasn't one of them. Steffi was a good mimic. She appeared to blow herself up to Bob Schapiro's size and said, "Sixmillionsixmillionsixmillion."

Erich said, "Did you see Ruth let the cuff of her sleeve fall accidentally on purpose open, to show the numbers on her wrist?"

"Did that strike you as impolite of her?" asked Margot.

Steffi said, "*Na, aber die is immer so hochnäsig.*"

"*Hochnäsig* translates, literally, into 'high-nosed'. Interesting", Margot said to Gretel beside her, "that both languages place the seat of arrogance in the nose. Do you know the expression 'being snotty'?"

They had lost Steffi and Erich to a conversation of their own. Gretel had been studying Margot and now said, "You don't think we have the right to say Ruth Schapiro does anything wrong?"

"I think you're wrong about her being *hochnäsig*: It's not that she looks 'down her nose' at you, it's that there *is* no way for her *to* look. What is the right way for Ruth Schapiro, with the numbers on her wrist, to look at you?"

Gretel said, "That was not what I asked: you think *we* don't have the right to criticise *you*."

Margot understood Gretel to mean "we all" and "you all", and said, "That's right. I don't grant you the right. Notice", she added, "that you and I are now saying the things for which Rabbi Sam has no exercises." She turned to all her table companions and asked, "What did *you all* come for?"

"I know the answer," Gretel bitterly said. "We came for you to console us for having been terrible."

Margot looked affectionately at Gretel. She patted the girl's arm.

Margot had agreed to give a little recital on the upright, which had not only the look but the timbre of a barroom piano. She played the first prelude and fugue of *The Well-Tempered Clavier* with a smile in the direction of Gretel Mindel. Gretel, as the day advanced, had become weepy.

Afterwards, everybody followed Rabbi Sam upstairs for the Shabbat service. He had the Viennese visitors rise to be introduced to the congregation. "Bridges" was the theme of his sermon.

When they returned downstairs, the windowless meeting room was transformed. The little tables had been rearranged into one long table covered with a cloth. During the salad, Rabbi Sam had them go around the table and say how the workshop had changed their lives.

Konrad passed. Shoshannah had made friends. Her hope in the human capacity for reconciliation had been revived. Steffi vowed to let no anti-Semitic remark in her hearing go unchallenged. Both Jenny Birnbaum and Erich Radezki were going to make their reluctant mothers tell their stories. Fritz Cohn was thinking of retiring to Vienna. Ruth said, "Bob and I are going to live in Israel."

"I'm going to Israel," Gretel said. Her ticket was taking her not back to Vienna but to Jerusalem, where she was registered for six months at the university. "I'm going to study Hebrew," she said.

"I'm going for a week's visit to my daughter in Los Angeles," said Margot. "Then I'll come home and practise the piano."

During the chicken, with vegetable garnish, Rabbi Sam announced his plan for another workshop under the auspices of Father Sebastian's church. He hoped the New York bridge-builders would come to Vienna and participate.

"I will come," said Shoshannah.

"I want my mom to go," said Jenny, and Fritz Cohn supposed that by that time he might have an apartment in Vienna.

During the chocolate layer cake, Father Sebastian rose. He had a request to make of the Viennese exiles.

"I'm not an exile," Ruth Schapiro said.

"Write a letter to Vienna. Tell us what you think about us," said Father Sebastian.

Red-headed Ruth Schapiro with the number on her wrist said, "I don't think about you."

"Come! Come to the workshop!" Gretel said to Margot. "Come and stay in my apartment."

"Thank you," Margot said. "I don't know that I'll be going back to Vienna."

Gretel came to help Margot look for her coat. She said, "Forgive me!"

"What for?" asked Margot. "I don't know that you've done anything wrong."

The girl held Margot's coat for her and wept and said, "I'm studying Hebrew!"

"I've forgotten mine," Margot said.

Gretel was watching Margot put her first arm into the first sleeve and the other arm into the other sleeve and felt time running out, and here came Father Sebastian to reinforce the invitation to Vienna and he shook Margot's hand goodbye, and Margot shook hands with Erich and with Steffi. "Goodbye, young Jenny. Goodbye Schapiros!" She embraced them. "Goodbye Shoshannah, goodbye Fritz." Everybody was shaking hands with everybody except for Konrad Hohenstauf, who had not come to join in the adieus by the door, or the plum-coloured turban, who had left without anybody noticing. "And thank you, Rabbi Rosen!" Margot said as she walked out.

"*Sei wieder gut!*" Gretel called after her.

It came to Margot Groszbart that she had not said goodbye to Gretel Mindel and she meant to – she thought she was going to turn around and wave to her, however she kept walking.

Divorce

Lilly is thinking about the morning, a month or so after the final decree, when she called Henry and said, "Can you remember exactly *why* we got divorced?"

"You always think things can be explained exactly," said Henry.

"Oh, really!" she said. "Is this one of the things that I 'always' think?"

"If you want to argue with me, you'll have to call back after I've had my coffee," said Henry.

"Anything else I 'have' to do?" she said and hung up.

Lilly remembers that it was the day their friends Jane and Johnny were in town. "It's *my* fault," Lilly had said to them. "Henry and I tried three and a half minutes worth of counselling, and I told the shrink that I'm a nag. Henry would bring me my coffee in one hand and carry his coffee in the other, and I'd nag him to use a tray and he always said he would but he never did." The shrink said, "Sounds like a good deal for both of you: Henry got to go on doing what he was doing and you could go on nagging."

"How's that again?" asked Johnny.

Jane said, "The two of you are not playing by the rules. You're supposed to blame *each other*!" Jane and Johnny had looked in on Henry in his temporary bachelor digs. "Henry says, it's all *his* fault. Says he knows it annoys the hell out of you that he keeps editing everything you say. Doesn't know why he keeps doing it."

"Yes, well," said Lilly. "Came the day when Henry sent his wedding ring to the laundry and I threw mine out the window."

"You what!" said Jane and Johnny.

"Not on purpose. Henry took off his ring when he went to wash up, to prevent it going down the drain. He said he put it in the pocket of his shirt and forgot about it. It must have got sent with the wash. I had lost some weight, because I remember my wedding ring felt loose. I was opening the window and knew the moment it went out. Henry and I took the elevator down and walked the sidewalk and looked for it."

Lilly's life continued in the old apartment, but Henry's job had required his relocating in London. Both had remarried and had grown children. There was no occasion for them to have connected with each other's family, so it wasn't until this January that Lilly heard of Henry's death the previous November. It shook her. Lilly had not been aware of thinking much or often about him, but his being dead makes a difference. She didn't know that she had relied on Henry's being alive. It troubles Lilly that she has gone about for three months in a world that Henry has not been in.

It's not that Lilly is looking for the wedding ring she threw out of the window some forty years ago.

Of course Lilly does not believe that a ring – it was a nice hand-hammered one – would have been lying out there all this time where anyone could have found and walked away with it, but she does not cross the sidewalk toward her front door without letting her eye skim the gutter, the building line where the wall meets the ground, these unevennesses in the surface (evidence of our deteriorating infrastructure) and the grouting that separates the asphalt squares, for the lost glimmer of gold.

Pneumonia Chronicles

My pre-existing condition was being ninety-two years old and, by taking every care to isolate me from Covid 19, my anxious children had isolated me from themselves and could not know that I had stopped eating. Nor did I know that I was ill when I called to ask Dr P. if there existed, and if she might prescribe me, a pill to instigate appetite.

When I was a child and got ill, my mother called Dr Schey. His doctor's bag had a wide mouth and he let me snap it open and shut. Dr Schey sat on the side of my bed, poked my stomach, listened to my back, looked in my ears and made me well again. It may be my old European awe of doctors, but I wonder what Dr P. asked me, or what I might have said that translated into the appearance, at my door, of a masked medical technician with an EKG apparatus and, before the end of that same morning, the ambulette. I thought it would bring me back home that same evening but it took me to Emergency, where I tested negative for Covid-19 and was transferred to a hospital room. A non-Covid pneumonia kept me for two weeks with a tube attached to my back draining fluid out of my chest cavity.

The plastic water cups on the table between my and my roommate's bed fell over of their insubstantiality. When I filled one with water, it fell over. Among the wires attached to the TV remote and other instruments the uses of which I was never going to disentangle, I found the call button. Nobody came to clean up the wet mess I had created.

I did not see my roommate's face, but through a gap in the translucent curtain suspended from the ceiling I watched the elegant, pale brown hands in motion; they kept me conscious of the human presence that could not help overhearing the answers I made the Intake Nurse who wanted me to remember three words she was going to say: "Gate". "Street". "Dog". Yes, I know my birth date. I know what year this is, what day of the week. I know where I am. Was she asking me if I ever considered cutting myself? No! Did I have the feeling that life was not worth living? Only as long as my back was hurting. Could I spell "world" backwards? Did I remember the three words? "Gate". "Street". "Dog".

My roommate and I are alone. Her conversation on the other side of the curtain is pitched so low I can't make out what she is saying, but I take it as reproof of my own full-voiced, my self-conscious responses to the Intake Nurse.

Six o'clock? Is this morning or evening? Have I been asleep? My neighbour is still talking while her hands wrap an apple into her white top sheet. She unwraps and rewraps the apple, wraps, unwraps and rewraps her bare left foot. She rewraps the apple and unwraps it, talking continually in that voice below the volume of human speech, evidently not on the telephone. My roommate is a loony talking to herself and her hand is reaching over to my bed for my black zippered bag; she wraps my bag in her sheet. My gasp has alerted the nurse, who rescues and returns my property.

Evening and morning, another day. My roommate is quiescent, not talking. Is she asleep? Has she been asleep all day? They come and wheel her out of the room. The story in my head tells me my loony roommate is dead. The nurse says, "No, they are moving her into another room," but isn't that what she would tell me? I will never know if, in the course of the day, this human being died in the bed beside me.

"I'm Brenda," my new roommate introduces herself.

"I'm Lore." They have put my clothes and things into a zippered plastic bag and moved me into another room on the same floor. Brenda is from New Jersey. I'm from Vienna. Brenda is a retired nurse. When the Floor Nurse comes into the room, the two women squeal in recognition. They used to work together! How long since they closed down St Vincent's? Brenda and I are fated to overhear each other's phone conversations with our doctors and with each other's children, who, in these Covid times, are not allowed to visit. I am moved to hear Brenda talking to her daughter. "Love, you," she says.

Brenda and I philosophise, "Everybody has their ups and downs. You know what I'm saying?" Brenda says.

"It is what it is," I respond. Brenda is dressed to go home. Her daughter is waiting for her down in reception. We will remember each other, we tell each other.

My next roommate is in pain. She cries, she weeps and asks "God! Why? Why? Why?" They come and they wheel her away before there is an answer, nor do I see my fourth roommate's face. When not quarrelling with the nurse or with herself, she sings in a reedy voice. Her complex melodies rise and fall at intervals that my ear does not expect or understand. She, too, is gone.

My roommate Anne was moved in while I was asleep. She is a tall African-American woman, seventy-four years old, she tells me. I'm ninety-two, I tell her.

We are both grandmothers. I admire and envy Anne's upright walk with her cane. I use a walker. I give Anne my banana and she passes me what is better, I guess, than no coffee at all. The good and true coffee my son Jacob leaves for me in reception is not heart-healthy and has been confiscated. Anne keeps track of the things for which I'm constantly searching my white bedscape. "Where, where, where is my call button?"

"It's on the other side of your knees," Anne tells me.

"What did I do with my phone?"

"You put it in your bag."

Thank you, Anne.

Transportation and corridors. The X-ray machine, like one half of a grey elephant, comes right to my beside, into my hospital room, but I will have to be transported to the CT scan, the MRI, the echocardiogram and ultrasound. Transportation has its own department and is short-handed. I have to wait for the two orderlies to come and wheel my bed, with me inside it, along the long, gleaming-white corridors. I have made use, in a story, of this spatial eternity where what is before you differs in no way from where you have been or what you are passing.

Why do the two masked blue uniforms believe that the undifferentiated and unpeopled corridors will have an end, or that the doors they remotely open and push me through will take us where we are going? But they know the geography and which corner to round to get to the elevators that take us up – or is it down – to the floor where we cross the covered bridge that connects with the other building's identical white corridors to the Department of Radiology. When they leave me to wait outside the door, they have not yet resolved the problem the younger one is having with the new girlfriend.

The procedure. The masked, blue-uniformed CT scan operator projects me, feet forward, into a large metal doughnut. It talks. It tells me when to breathe and when to hold my breath. The CT scan operator has wheeled me back into the corridor and left me where I understand, that I will wait for Transportation to take me back to my room.

Night and day, the hospital is lighted as with Klieg lights and nothing in this uniform whiteness arrests the eye. If there are doors they must open from the other side, for here are no visible handles or knobs. Nor is there any sound in the CT scan room. The CT scan operative has gone home.

Waiting. I left my watch on the bedside table in the room thinking there might be nowhere to put it during the procedure. Waiting for a bus or for the elevator, for the doctor to come, or for Transportation to take you back to your room, the minute is as long as the five, as the fifteen minutes which are equivalent to an hour, the unit of time that does not have any end.

There is someone – someone is walking, a man in civvies. I call him, tell him my name, ask him to please tell someone, to please remind Transportation, that I am outside the CT Scan

Room, waiting, have been waiting and waiting in this corridor. But I am not the man's business. He says to wait till Transportation has two people available. The man in civvies has somewhere he has to go. He is walking away. He is gone.

There will be no other human sighting. What would happen if I screamed, out loud, under the Klieg lights, if I made a loud noise. I do not scream, and they have come, the two or two other masked blue-uniforms who know the geography to the covered bridge and along these corridors, through the several doors, and take me back to my room.

A scream. That night, or the next or another night, somebody is screaming. "What's that?" I ask the nurse who is taking my vitals. What I want is for her to deny that I am hearing what I do not want, what I am indignant to have to bear to hear. "It's the pain," the nurse says. This is the human scream that has lost all reserve, all shame and sense of self, and it goes on for minutes on end and someone needs to go and do something, for this ought not to be allowed, ought never to be heard and I then remember, I recognise the human howl that Ivan Ilyich's wife and daughter, and the daughter's fiancé, and the schoolboy son, had to hear him screaming for a night and a day.

It has stopped, has it? There must have been a moment when the screaming ceased.

The nurses. Today's medicine does not seek to cure the sick by bloodletting, but the hospital day begins with the nurse sticking me with a needle which collapses my unstable vein so that she has to stick me a second and third time or more to fill three vials with enough blood for the doctors to know what is going on inside me and keep me alive into my nineties without, like Dr Schey, sitting on the edge of my bed.

The nurse with the needle checks my vitals. She is an RN, or Registered Nurse, There is a CRN, or Certified Registered Nurse. I do not know what the BN Nurse does, but the QIEN is a Quality Improvement Executive Nurse. In the hospital's daily operation we meet my friend the Intake Nurse, the Charge Nurse, the Floor Nurse and an Assistant

Nurse Manager, none of them to be mistaken for the practical nurses who have too much to do to respond when I ring and ring and ring the call button because I need to go to the bathroom.

Here is a truism: there is, always has been and will always be, the nice or good nurse, and there will always, on a scale of one to ten, be the other nurses.

The good nurse says, "That's OK, baby," when I apologise for knocking over yet another cup of water.

"That's all right, mama," she says and straightens the sheet that has bunched under my sore back; her hands are my friends. Would I like a pillow under my neck?

The other, the nurse who is not answering my bell, does not, for the most part, mean to be mean. She has too much to do and what she wants is to do any damn thing rather than take me to the bathroom again, which I can understand. She will, when she can, do what is required, which may not include hearing me when I make a joke. She chooses not to smile.

Surveys: I propose to engage in a minor act of civil disobedience by not answering surveys.

How often, during your hospital visit, did nurses treat you with courtesy and respect:

Always, Usually, Often, Sometimes, Never? YES.
On a scale of one to ten? NO.

My favourite nurse and new friend. Call him Elisha. A bearded black thirty-year-old. Elisha taught me how to access the hospital's Wi-Fi on my iPad and asked me if I knew the story about this Lady and the pet dog.

Yes! My favourite Chekhov story.

Elisha came into my room whenever he had a moment, and we talked Chekhov.

One of his teachers, he told me, put him onto Cornel West. Cornel West put Elisha onto community college which put him onto Chekhov. Elisha had taken a class on the Bible and was reading Robert Alter's translation of Deuteronomy.

Here is where I got to name-drop: "Robert Alter was one of my teachers."

"You know Robert Alter!" cried Elisha.

Came the day I dressed to go home. My daughter Beatrice was waiting for me down in reception.

Elisha and I email. Elisha got me back to reading Chekhov. When he asks what he should read next, I put him onto Tolstoy's *The Death of Ivan Ilyich*.

Bedroom Lesson

My apartment is on the twelfth floor and the window across from my bed faces due east. For years – decades – I looked for ways to prevent the morning sun from shining into my light-sensitive eyes and giving me a daily headache. Why didn't I simply move the bed, or put up curtains? Distrust "simply", which would seem to promise that moving something, or putting something somewhere, will take care of what is wrong.

My bedroom is blessed with advantages: beside the east window across from my bed, it has twin windows to the south, a walk-in closet and the door into the bathroom. There is no wall to which the bed could be moved – or moved so as not to face a window the light of which would give me a headache. The project was to find curtains to keep the light out. I tried materials of varying weights and thicknesses, with the fabric doubled or lined. Each took time to research, purchase, to install and discover that it did no better than what had gone before. German speaks of the *Tücke des Objekts*, the spite of the inanimate object. I don't know that one can speak of light as an "object" but I experienced its malice. The more effectively the newest curtain prevented light from coming through the windows' panes, the more it concentrated the inevitable strips of light down the right and left edges, to irritate my photophobia.

If I made anything like a decision, I don't remember, cannot point to a day or the moment I acknowledged defeat and abandoned the search for curtains. There was the year I put up the handsome, modern vertical blinds that didn't so much as promise to keep the the light out; and they rattled. It is long since I replaced them with regular blinds.

They are a nuisance to clean, but I have come to admire the horizontal lines with which, let all the way down in the open position at all times, they organise the world outside my three windows.

These days I wake to one-hundred-eighty degrees of the dawning sky: the two south windows give me the expanse of morning sky over New York, my adopted city. Past the water tower on the nearby roof and across the massed variety of box and pencil-shaped high-rises, I can see the Empire State Building.

Beyond the east window, a new thirty-two-storey glass tower has changed the view from my bed. It has cut a piece out of the sky but leaves me a cleft where, on clear mornings, I watch the sunrise. Derrida undertook what he knew not to be impossible – to chart a constantly changing sunset, inch by inch, moment to moment. I'll tell you that dawn is not rosy-fingered, but comes in the palest and the sharpest greens, and orange that turns gold and for long moments burns in the glass towers like unobstructed fire. And the photophobia? How is it that my old age does not suffer headaches? Is it that I have stopped quarrelling and no longer want to prevent light from shining? Today I invite it in by every window and it diffuses throughout my room and does me no harm.

Relative Time

Albert Einstein and Shakespeare's Rosalind agree that time travels at "divers paces" with diverse persons. Rosalind says that time trots with the young maid toward her wedding day and gallops with the thief to the gallows. I propose to illustrate the theory that time moves faster or slower relative to non-accelerating observers who are waiting for someone with whom they have an appointment at an agreed upon time and place; and to analyse the different speeds at which diverse types move en route to this meeting.

There are, I believe, three types of time travellers: those who are always late; those who cannot help getting there before the appointed time; and the admirable, the enviable, members of a human subspecies who arrive where they are going when they are supposed to get there, no sweat.

Take the third first. Call him Horatio, for perhaps it is the man that is not passion's slave who, without having to think anything about it, knows how long it will take him to get dressed, and when to leave the house.

He correctly estimates the time things take and how far space stretches between where he is and where he needs to be. And more: Horatio has faith that the immediate future is not likely to put a roadblock across his path in the nature, say, of a tsunami; that he will not fall down his front steps nor reach the corner and, realising that he has forgotten the piece of paper with the address, needs to run back and look for it.

The second is the type of which, being my mother's daughter, I am myself an instance. I have over a long life aggregated many hours walking round the block, or finding a nearby place to drink an unneeded cup of coffee because I have arrived too early.

My mother, who assumed the broken leg at the bottom of the stairs, the Flood, and that the address on the piece of paper will turn out to have shifted its location and geography, reckoned an additional half-hour – better say an hour. If it was going to take her forty-five minutes – say an hour – to get to a two o'clock appointment, she had better start out by twelve-thirty, say twelve noon to make sure.

Now just in case something happens to prevent her leaving at twelve, she should, to be on the safe side, leave at eleven. Starting an hour or two before setting out, this type of traveller experiences anxiety like a low roiling in the chest and a churning belly, for the tsunami, the fractured leg, and the lost address are more likely than not.

Our final time traveller is Beatrice, one of the favourite people in my world, who has promised that she will be at my place at two. I have known Beatrice since the day she was born, but I do not know if she knows she will be an hour, an hour and a half, late. What she does know is that I assume she is going to be late, which annoys her.

Never doubt that our two o'clock appointment is most honorably fixed in Beatrice's mind and that two o'clock is the hour at which she intends to arrive as promised and agreed upon. And it is two o'clock, indeed, or ten or twenty minutes before or after two, that her inner clock tells her to get dressed in order to go into her backyard to gather the beautiful things she is going to bring me – the little tomatoes, a bag of basil leaves and the cucumber. There is no cucumber like the one Beatrice will fresh-pick for me in her backyard after she takes the dog for a quick run and, trusting there will be no traffic to hamper the forty-five-minute drive to my place, and that she will have no trouble finding parking, she rapidly answers a couple of emails that have been on her conscience and, having remembered that the washing needs to be taken out of the machine and hung to dry, Beatrice gets into her car and arrives – what in my time-space experience is an hour, an hour and a half late.

What to do? Beatrice must learn to manage her time so as to be on time, which she is so entirely willing but equally entirely unable to do. Or must I learn not to mind, to recognise that it does not matter in the greater or lesser scheme of things whether Beatrice is or is not going to be late? But that's what I am unable to do.

We need a moral: let us be patient with each other and with ourselves, and suffer the diverse paces at which we move through one another's time and space.

Ladies' Zoom

"Remember the last time we met," Bessie said, "we had an impromptu, a – a – not a shivah, of course – what's the word I'm not going to be able to remember for sitting around telling Lotte stories?"

"I think", Farah said, "we were sorry and feeling bad that we didn't visit her in Green – Green what was the place called? Not Green Parks, not Green Fields. Green Place? Green Peace? Green something, nice enough, I guess, way out in the boonies."

"Why do we guess it was nice," Bessie said, "when we never managed to round up a car to drive ourselves to see her in the – what do they call the kind of – the – what do you call the living for old people that Lotte's son moved her into. The other son who came up from Chicago..?"

"...Whose name," Ruth said, "is the same as – what's the name of the character by what's his name? – dear heaven, am I going to forget who – wrote the fellow who wakes up on his back – it's not clear what species of bug, waving his six legs in the air..."

Bridget said, "I am always going to find the neatest, briefest way to signal and apologise the next time I lose yet another word..."

"If", Farah said, "you can locate the words to make the apology."

"The trick", Bessie said, "will be to not embark on a sentence one hasn't the vocabulary to get to the end of."

"Or confess defeat," said Ilka, "and give up talking altogether."

"Oh don't, don't, don't," Hope said. "Oh, let us not stop talking."

The next time – it was in response to their several children's anxieties – Ruth offered to try to host ladies' lunch on Zoom. "It might be a good idea to hold up a hand to signal when you have something to say," she told them. "We have forty minutes, and another forty if I can figure out how to work it."

They could be guaranteed to quarrel with the technology. "We're talking to little movies of ourselves instead of with each other."

Only Farah held up a hand to say, "It's this blessed technology that lets me carry Kafka and all of Jane Austen and *King Lear*, and *What Maisie Knew* in my handbag and make the letters large enough to read."

Bessie had an agenda: "Are we, all of us, wanting to clean up – to simplify what we leave our children to deal with? I have files of papers that I will never read again but can't throw out because I would have to read them to know that what I'm throwing out is what I would never read again."

Bridget said, "After Lotte died, I was going to erase her entry from my address book, and then I didn't. Could not."

All the little moving pictures on the computer screen nodded their heads up and down and Bessie's mouth said, "I know, I know. I have a drawer of decades-old address books full of dead people that I keep not throwing out. Dead or alive, it turns out one cannot throw people away."

Ilka, said, "One can't, or one doesn't. Even people I don't remember, whose names I don't know. Guys, can you put up with yet one more of my backstories?"

"Go ahead." The little pictures on their computers nodded their heads.

"My Mutti's favourite summer Sundays," Ilka said, "were spent in the Vienna baths, great parks with one or more swimming pools with changing rooms, and I think – I try to remember, now there's not a soul living in the world I can ask – that there was a place where we ate? Or did Mutti bring a picnic? For the children there was a sweet red bubbly drink – the *Kracherl*. I have an album, and there are boxes of snapshots that have come with me on every leg of the emigration – the rows of laughing cousins on benches, with their spouses and children; I know names – Maxl, Miklos, Karl, Ditta, Mila – but I can't tell which is which. They pose at the edge of the pool. Who is the comedian making like an ape? Several identical copies of the snapshot of a man I don't think I ever met, that I don't throw away. What vestige of the idea of the sacred prevents us from erasing a human person?"

"Is it the enigma", Hope said, "of being erased?"

And then their forty minutes were up.

ACKNOWLEDGEMENTS

My late husband David said that the editor's function was to understand where the writer wanted to go and to help her arrive. For caring about my work I thank Natania Jansz at Sort Of Books, Valerie Merians of Melville House and Cressida Leyshon for the decades at *The New Yorker*. Without their friendship this book would not be what it is.

Lore Segal, New York, January 2023

PUBLICATION HISTORY

Lore Segal published her first *Ladies' Lunch* story in the *New Yorker* in 2007 and the most recent, *Soft Sculpture*, in summer 2022. For this collection, she has written three new stories and brought them together into a sequence with earlier tales featuring the same characters, published in the *New Yorker* and elsewhere. The *Other Stories* include three stories and three new, previously unpublished pieces of memoir.

A number of these stories were collected in *The Journal I Did Not Keep* (Melville House Publishing, 2019), an anthology of Lore Segal's writings that also features excerpts from her novels and essays.

LADIES' LUNCH

1 Ruth, Frank and Dario, *New Yorker, 2020*
2 Days of Martini and Forgetting, *Epiphany, 2018*
3 How Lotte Lost Bessie, *Fifth Wednesday Journal, 2016*
4 The Arbus Factor, *New Yorker, 2007*
5 Soft Sculpture, *New Yorker, 2022*
6 Mother Lear, *Previously unpublished, 2022*

7 Around the Corner You Can't See Around,
   New Yorker, 2021
8 Ladies' Lunch, *New Yorker, 2017*
9 Sans Teeth, Sans Taste, *Previously unpublished, 2022*

OTHER STORIES

Dandelion, *New Yorker, 2019*
Making Good, *American Scholar, 2008*
Divorce, *Egg Review, 2017*

Pneumonia Chronicles, *Previously unpublished, 2022*
Bedroom Lesson, *Previously unpublished, 2022*
Relative Time, *Previously unpublished, 2022*

Ladies' Zoom, *Previously unpublished, 2022*

Also by Lore Segal

Fiction

Other People's Houses (1964)
Lucinella (1976)
Her First American (1985)
Shakespeare's Kitchen (2007)
Half The Kingdom (2013)

The Journal I Did Not Keep (ANTHOLOGY, 2019)

Translations

Gallows Songs of Christian Morgenstern (1967)
The Juniper Tree and Other Tales from Grimm (1973)
The Book of Adam to Moses (1987)
The Story of King Saul and King David (1991)

Children's Books

Tell Me a Mitzi (1970)
All the Way Home (1973)
Tell Me a Trudy (1979)
The Story of Old Mrs Brubeck and How She Looked for
Trouble and Where She Found Him (1981)
The Story of Mrs Lovewright and Purrless Her Cat (1985)
Morris the Artist (2003)
Why Mole Shouted and Other Stories (2004)
More Mole Stories and Little Gopher, Too (2005)